Hunters of the Mist

If the doors of perception were cleansed every thing
would appear to man as it is: Infinite.   William Blake

Other Books by this author:

Psychic Nazi Hunter
(The Extraordinary Biography of Alan Wood-Thomas)

End of Times Trilogy (Sci Fi)
Eat Your Fill - Eat Your Religion - Eat Your God

The Book of Number Trilogy (Mantic Science)
Workbook - Interpretations - Practitioner Guide

Jermimiah Versus the Grabblesnatch (Fiction - Myth)

The Divinity Dice Series (Mantic Science)
Decimal Dice - Divinity Dice - Book of Aspects - Pythagorean Patterns

Ratology: Way of the Un-Dammed (Non-Fiction)

Ratology II: Who Gives a Rats? (Non-Fiction)

Fragments of the Mirror (Short Stories)

Witch Hunter and other stories (Short Stories)

Water: More Precious than Gold (Non-Fiction)

The Borringbar War (3 Day Auto Biography)

Hello Planet Earth (Short Stories - Modern Myth)

Rome Too / Rome Tree (Parody)

Parables of Geoff (Biography)

The Wand (Fantasy)

Wolves of Planet Hope (Sci Fi)

Planet Aqua (Sci Fi)

Available on Amazon or at
www.laddertothemoon.com.au

Hunters of the Mist

COPYRIGHT 2021 - Ladder to the Moon Publications
Author: Ecallaw Leachim
ISBN: 978-0-6452723-0-7

All enquiries via Email to: qrcaustralia@gmail.com
Published by Ladder to the Moon Publications.

https://www.law.cornell.edu/treaties/berne/overview.html

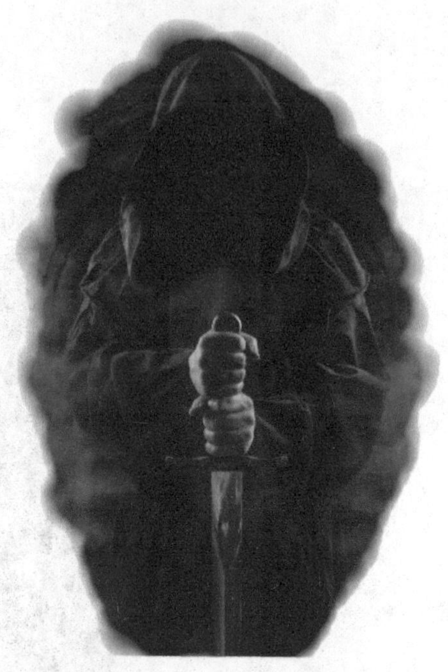

Hunters of the Mist

Ecallaw Leachim

The time is the distant future. A mining ship has returned from an extended tour of the outer reaches and finds the Earth is all but destroyed. Some sort of cataclysm has descended and the sun itself no longer shines upon the land. The crew of the Canter discovers a way to clear the air, to allow in sunlight, but a suffocating mist still covers most of the land, a mist that houses creatures of horror who seek to dominate all that come near them.

Small pockets of humanity remain, but it is like the stone age. Jack Blake undertakes an arduous program, one that runs for decades, slowly educating the primitive people to perform the most basic tasks of civilization. And through it all, the Gregorians, the witch hunters track into the mist and free the land from control by the aliens that have taken residence in it.

But of course, there is far more to it than meets the eye!

Hunters of the Mist

"Time is but the stream I go a-fishing in. I drink at it; but while I drink I see the sandy bottom and detect how shallow it is. Its thin current slides away, but eternity remains."
Henry David Thoreau

Witch Hunters

The only truth we truly know is that we do not know what will come. There is but ONE certainty, change - anything can occur and this is as true of planets as it is for individuals. It is most certainly true for a civilization. We cannot be certain if we humans will survive the next stage: A virus might wipe us out, a super volcano may reduce us to a permanent ice age, a comet might strike - as it did to end the reign of the dinosaurs. But while we live and breathe as a people, what will never change is the human will - to survive, to understand, to grow.

Presuming we survive the change, of course.

The cold, grey mist clung to your bones like sadness to a forlorn lover. A chill wind grazed the remnants of nature as it struggled to survive. Bleak and forlorn, these outlands were to be avoided by all sensible folk, not just for the sunless, empty reaches filled with strange creatures, but because these were the areas controlled by the witches.

The Gregorians were the only defense against these black hearts and a training day such as this put life and limb on the line. "It's not just the witches out here boys," the instructor whispered, "there are also their monsters, things they create from the angst and suffering of the people. The witches draw on energy to live, vampires of a sort, and they use this to make their protectors. You know why we are here, I also know you are scared, any sensible person would be - but be warned, the scent of fear is what draws them in."

Pherial Artrim looked at his new recruits. It was always the same, eager, scared faces, keen to be one of the protectors. Not that he was pessimistic, but the facts were that most of them would soon enough be dead. He sighed, for the present, best to keep talking before they had to go into the silence. "Now, you might think a witch was vulnerable when she sleeps, but no, that is when her creatures are out. This is why we hunt them during our day - for this is the time they walk their lands. We are not going for a hard target, just a basic witch such as lives here on the outskirts. Do as you have been taught and, with any luck, you will soon discover for yourself the joy of releasing the land from their grasp."

He paused to make sure they were paying attention. "Remember, there is only ONE way to kill a witch, you have to net her mid-spell."

Master Artrim had been a witch hunter for some eighty or more years. You lose count, but a long time. Every year, a new batch of recruits like this had to face their first challenge, and he knew more than a few would fail, either in heart or by the blood. Soon, some creature would be licking the last vestige of life from one or more of these lads as they lay on the cold, barren ground.

He didn't pay a lot of attention to the recruits at this point. Out of the ten he had with him, he expected that only one would make the grade, and that one rarely lived more than four years. Cold, hard statistics stopped him from forming any bonds of affection. Three would be eaten by the wild, three would run in terror back to their mothers, to live in shame their whole life. Three would just kill themselves after they see the pointlessness of their existence echoed here in this parody of life. ONE, if he or she were lucky, would live four years before being caught and turned into a Whyte.

Fooking witches, he hated them with such a passion. Master Artrim was the greatest hunter who had ever lived, having personally killed over three hundred of them, five of them Twitches, the High Witches that controlled whole swathes of territory with their spells. He had brought countless acres of sunlight to grateful farmers and townsfolk.

"This is the battleground, lads. You kill the local witch, you release her spell casting, the clouds breach, and sunlight streams through. The sunlight is what heals the land and drives out the evil, not us. Our job is just to kill the bitches who bring the grey mist. Remember this, nothing else is the enemy, not even the creatures. Only the Witch is important, and there is only one way to catch her - in mid-spell. How do we do this, you ask?" Pherial holds up a coin, a simple coin of the realm.

"A witch cannot resist the lure of a coin rolled in front of her. No one knows why, no one cares why. A witch sees a coin, and she pauses her incantations to pick it up. This is the ONLY time she is vulnerable."

He pauses, does he bother to waste breath to tell them more? They all knew the facts, only one of them would end up being worth something. "But remember, witches are drawn to coins of differing quality. If you want a higher-up one, you need a silver coin, and for a Twitch, you need pure gold. They will not be drawn to anything less. Plus the Twitch, she needs to physically pick up that coin. It has to touch her skin. They are impossible to catch without the metal poisoning her first."

"But you caught FIVE. How?" one of the boys asks.

"Aye, here's the rub laddie. No Twitch will fall for a trap or a dummy like we will set today. You have to offer YOURSELF, because they know the difference between the fakes and real humans. Your WILL has to defeat them, your pure hatred, your pure determination has to override theirs, and you have to slap that damn coin onto their skin. Your pure, unadulterated COURAGE is the only thing that will defeat a Twitch, lads. You need to find an impossible courage to win - I found mine from inside my hatred, because of what one of those bitches did to my family. You will find yours where you can."

The most promising recruit was Tomic Suras, from the Midlands. "I have heard the tales, Master Artrim, but I cannot help be thinking that by now they would realize the trick and bait US instead. What is to stop two witches knowing we are about, and allowing one to look like she is vulnerable. We go in, we die. Makes sense to me."

"Aye, it DOES make sense. What doesn't is why they never learn. One day, you might be right, one day they may work together and defeat us, but until that day let us be grateful that all the venom and spite and bitterness that goes into making a witch makes them as unpalatable to each other as they are to us. Don't forget this lads, each witch hates her sisters. Each witch wants to control more witches, more territory, and breed more mist. This is why we keep beating them back at the fringe, to stop them expanding and eating up the good farmlands."

He signaled a pause and cocked his ear to listen. No, nothing yet. "Soon we will not be able to speak. They have acute hearing these things do and they be listening for their supper. Now, from the density of the fog, I can tell we are coming into the range of one of them. A low-grade fringe dweller like what we are hunting is not particularly strong, but the deeper you go in, the more powerful, the more paranoid, and the more dangerous they become."

Jimith Tyler asks, "Is it true, Master Artrim, that when a Twitch dies it releases whole territories back to the farmers?"

"It is Jimith. I am a wealthy man from all the taxes they pay me as a result, a very wealthy man, and my children should I have them will have an easy life. But this is not why I am here. Nor am I here for accolades or medals, though I have plenty of both. I am here to kill witches. Nothing else is in my mind or heart. I am CONSUMED by the desire to end this blight upon our people."

A boy who was certain to fail puts up a querulous hand. The Master looks over and nods, knowing the poor lad was driven out here by his rapacious stepmother. She wanted a piece of the hunter taxes and was happy for the boy to pay with his life to make hers easier. What was his name? Ah, yes, "Cleath, first, asking permission to speak is a kindergarten habit you must wash from your mind. Second, we know you do not want to be here. It is no shame to leave and run back home. Live child, you have no chance out here and you know it."

"Master," he finds the courage to speak. "Master Artrim, surely the witches were once human like us. What turns them? What changes their hearts to become the evil they embrace?"

"A philosopher are you then, lad? Many have asked this same question, boy. Many have gone out with perfect intentions to research, to understand, to discover what aberration caused this foul stench to creep over our blighted lands. They have gone out in fine carriages with armies to defend them, along with wise men. And if they survived at all, they came back broken, missing teeth or hands or feet." Master Artrim knew this well. His own father, may he rest in peace, tried to find out what caused this infection.

"My own father tried. Somehow he got permission to speak with a Twitch, can you believe? This was in the early days, before the mist had spread so far, before the Gregorians were formed. She turned his mind into madness, removed one eye, one toe, one finger, and his cock before sending him back to my mother, an utterly broken, insane man. She did this ON PURPOSE! (he shouts) She did this to show us we were powerless. She did this to break our spirits.

"That Twitch took a good man and made him utterly useless, like this land around us. So, young Cleath, ask these questions if you will. Go speak with these witches if you wish, but expect to end up like my poor Da. WHY do you think I hate them so damn much? WHY do you think I hunt them night and day? WHY do you think I am out here training the next crew of Witch Hunters?" He nodded at them to silence then, for his passions had stirred the mist, calling in a witch.

He whispered, "Do you feel it, lads? My passion is bait, they cannot resist it. My hatred draws them to me. All we have to do is lay a trap, a place where my coin can roll easily in front of them. Now you must be completely silent and stay near, and just watch. Do NOT try to tackle this thing on your own. You all have your copper net? (the boys nod in the affirmative) Good."

Master Artrim looks at his map and sees that nearby an old village once stood. Excellent, that will have a hall where they can set up. Silently he signals them to move forward and soon they are in the ruins of what was once a thriving community. All gone, only the shells of buildings and the ghosts of the past remain. The village hall was battered and beaten, yet it still stood - the perfect trap.

He whispered to them, "Your fear is like a beacon to the witch near here, even now she is licking the mist, finding her way to us. Witches feed on negative passions: hate, anger, lust, vanity. This is food for them, and they can never have enough. We need to set up a dummy in the middle of the hall (He pulls out an inflatable mock-up of a person, and using a small power pack, pumps it up.) I know it looks incredibly easy to tell the difference between this and a real human, but witches do not see as we do. What we do now is project all our negative feeling into this thing."

He places it into the middle of the hall, where it stands in an awkward posture, bobbing about in a mimicry of life. "Now lads, everything you have always hated, feared, or loathed - feel it, taste it, and IMAGINE it is in this dummy. The witch hungers for emotion and will home in on the fake, casting spells to capture its mind. That is when we can paralyze her with a coin, then net her. You got that?"

They all nod in sullen silence, close their eyes, and do what they had been trained for the last year to do. "Project your thoughts and feelings, lads, make them part of that dummy. Put all your hate of these vile creatures in there."

As promised, soon an ugly form of grey starts to gather at the door. It is a woman, of sorts. Matted hair, sallow skin, blank, white eyes, apparently devoid of pupils or iris. It was not particularly tall and looked incredibly fragile, but the boys knew, it was the MIND that took your will away and turned you into a vegetable. They kept focussing on the dummy, making IT the center of hatred and fear. Slowly, carefully, the thing moved closer, chanting the words of control under its breath. Deep in spell casting, feeling the food it needed so close, it was blind to the humans all around it.

Then the coin is released from Master Artrim's hands. It rolls on its edge, slowly towards the dummy. The witch's attention is drawn to it, her head tilts as if following its path. Then it tilts the other way, locked in fascination, like a bird frozen by the flickering pattern of the snake about to strike.

He leaps up, the Master has the net flying through the air to scoop up the Witch, but she is quick. Too quick for a low grade. Dammit, a TWITCH, the bitch was faking it, baiting THEM. She knew it was a training exercise and had come out for THEM. Master Artrim's hand reached for his pocket, to pull out the gold coin, the only thing that could trap a Twitch, but he was too late. She had his mind, she was already controlling his motions. All his will, all his hatred, all his fire burned and pushed her back. He had done this once, he had done this FIVE TIMES - she would not hold him.

He should have known, he should have sensed her and sent the boys back. The distraction of looking after them had covered up her presence. This was planned, this was organized, just as little Tomic had predicted.

Pherial Artrim was a fighter like no other. He had a will of pure iron, yet he could feel her beating him back, laughing, saying in his mind that she will do to HIM what she did to the father. Dammit, this was the one. This was the very start of things, the first accursed Twitch that mutilated his Da. He hated her more, drove her back with ever great waves of hate. But he was losing. She was strong, too strong.

But then, the miracle. Little Cleath walked up, sacrificing himself to save the Master. He walked right up to a TWITCH, the brave little soul. Master Artrim felt her control seeping away as she turned with fascination at the young boy. Tears were in his eyes, great sadness overwhelmed him as he reached out to her, "Why?" he asked, with pure, childlike, open-hearted curiosity. "Why do you do this? Do you have a name? Do you want to talk?"

The Twitch is frozen in place, wondering. Her head tilts to one side. She starts to speak, a witch never speaks to a human, they only consume them, but she does not eat his energy and leave him like a grey stalk. *She wants to speak?* Master Artrim needed no further assistance, he pulls his gold coin, slaps it on her forehead, which immediately immobilizes the creature, and nets it. "All of you, throw your nets! We need to cut off her electronic connection to the atmosphere. Everyone!" he commands.

They do, apart from Cleath, who has tears in his eyes, watching the creature scream and squeal as her power is captured and contained by the other boys. She collapses to the floor, a shattered wreck, howling in pain and fear. All around them, the mist starts to evaporate, the noiseless shuffling of death begins to depart the scene and blessed sunlight starts to filter through the clouds.

The light is poison to a Witch! She begins to decompose, evaporating like the mist it created, screaming and squealing the whole time - until silence. Sweet, blessed silence flows out, and in exchange, shafts of sunlight fall through the battered shutters of the hall. Steams of golden light dissolve the last of the witch's spell, and the land is freed from her curse.

Pherial cannot believe it, they are all alive, and little Cleath - he saved them all. How he did it, he had no idea, but the mere twig of a boy started down a damn TWITCH! He stood there with nothing but his courage and stared down a Twitch. He goes over to pick up the shaking, weeping lad, who is pale and weak from the challenge. "Boy, you saved us all. I don't know how, but you saved us all. Let's go up the tower in the church and see how much land you have earned for yourself!"

Cheering, with Master Artrim carrying the still weak child, the boys all rush to the high point, to look out over the lands. From up there they can see hundreds of acres of ruined countryside, bent trees, brown broken shrubs barely alive, but they can SEE them. The mist is gone for miles and miles around. There will be enough food from these fields to feed a thousand settlers!

But Cleath is not cheering, he is not even smiling. He whispers to himself, "She was so desperately alone. So desperately in need of love..."

Master Artrim hears his soft voice, and with his free hand, tenderly wipes the tears from his eyes. "Lad, who could have imagined that my father may have been right after all. I watched her, she could not penetrate your strange and unexplainable compassion, and in the end, she wanted it. That is what made her vulnerable. She took in a little of your love, rather than our hate, and it destroyed her."

Cleath looked up, a question in his eyes. "Do you think she would have turned? Do you think she could have left that space that made her a witch?"

Pherial smiled, "The very same questions my father asked. Lad, in all honesty, I believe it was only that you caught her by surprise that it worked. She tried to trap us, she was using our hatred for her as bait to draw US into her trap. Then she saw your courage, your faith, your kindness, and it forced her to shift gears, to recalibrate, just like when a normal witch sees a coin. I am not be thinking we will be so lucky twice, lad. But be at peace, you have freed the lands from her curse. And young Cleath - you are now a wealthy man, one who will be celebrated and praised for a hundred years."

"I didn't do this for the gold, or the glory," Cleath whispered, still deeply in shock.

"No true Witch Hunter does, lad. No true Witch Hunter does."

The boys have paid no attention to the conversation. They were too busy cheering as more mist rolled back from the edges. Little puffs of smoke blew up, and more land appeared. "How come Master Artrim? There seem to be small explosions of mist at the edges of the cleared lands, then more land is revealed."

Master Artrim looks up, "Ah, yes. The greatest sight for a Witch Hunter. This is because, in her dying moments, the Twitch called in all her creatures to save her. They are rushing blindly towards her call, but when they hit the sunlight, they are destroyed. She was a powerful one and being right on the edge of her territory, everything she created will be rushing in. This mist may well roll back another hundred miles. You lads can be proud, you have been witness to the most amazing capture and destruction of a Twitch and are now part of legend. Even better, we are still alive to speak of it! All your names will go down in the records of the greats."

Finally, Cleath is strong enough to stand, "And we all get a share of the bounty," he says. "We were all in this together, we all get a share."

The boys cheer wildly. Master Artrim smiles, and says, "Looks like you have gotten yourself your own hunting posse, young Cleath. Onwards then lads, let's get back to the guild hall and register the kill."

The old man nods to himself, deep in thought as they make their way back in clean, blessed sunlight. The death all around him is shriveling, recoiling from the brightness it is exposed to. He felt himself resting with his father's thoughts - *Life is so beautiful, why would anything willingly want to live in the shadows?* Was it possible they may one day understand these creatures?

But enough of thinking! On this magnificent day, this glorious day, he returns not just with a gift to his people, he brings back all the boys, and all of them heroes. No greater thing can he do than to clear the lands and raise the next generation to follow in his steps. This is a day of wonder, a day worthy of song, and like the sunshine that endlessly flows, his heart glows with the joy of life.

The Great Tor

The great Tor reached out above the trees, moving slowly along the road. Ever since the prophet gave this miracle of the old world to the quest, the young had galvanized into a small army of laborers, all working towards the one goal - bringing it to the edge of the blighted lands. This was a sign of glory to come, the human fighting back against the bleak threat of the witches.

It sailed like a ship on an ocean of leaves. The expedition leader watched with a grim satisfaction as the unseen youth on the road below played their part in the great drama. Finding the relic was one thing, lost in the barren lands, but bringing it out of there, to the edge of the green, to the place where it shall stand as the sentinel against the encroachment - This great task shall be sung in the halls of victory itself. Even the Gods will look in wonder at what their creation could achieve.

Ciera looks from the rise at the slow, ponderous movement of the monolith. It was like a God itself, one of the ancient ones returned to bring order and peace back to the world. The sacred gift of concrete, the elder had said, from a time long ago when man built ladders into the sky. Before the plague, before the ruination, at a time when the citadels of the ancestors rose in defiance of nature.

It was said man was punished for his vanity. Some believed the great tides that swept in and the earth quakes that shattered the cities were sent by the old gods, to bring man back to his truth. All that is known is that a once-great civilization was crushed, leaving the scattered remnants of tribes to fend for themselves in a dangerous world.

Slowly the land had healed, the forests regrew, and the people emerged from the scarred lands where they had subsisted on rodents and herbs. Inside a few generations the farms had been planted, the villages built, and the few animals that had survived brought into safety and bred to assist the rebirth. The tribes had listened to the old man, his word had been always true, and they emerged from the dust of ruin to form a new society, a better place.

He had heard that across the vast waters some of the ancients still existed, with their miraculous flying vehicles, but if this were truth, surely they would have come? No, it was but idle speculation. His world, the world of his people needed certainty, such as the Great Tor offered.

Here was truth, a symbol of the ancient days that they would mount at the fringe as a warning: *Come no further!*

The vast plains extended as far as the eye could see. But in the distance, the brown murk of the witches was now visible - This was where the journey ended. This was the truth, they must stop the invasion of evil into the sacred lands, the mist which destroyed all it came into contact with. But no more! This sacred relic would repel the curse, it was known.

It had only been a couple of generations since the witches appeared, eating up the fertile lands, ruining them, destroying human settlements, and occupying them with all manner of foul creatures. They had made great inroads until the Witch Hunters, the Gregorians, were formed to fight them back. But was it enough? For every yard gained in one direction, two were lost in another.

But with the great icon of man, the Tor, they would succeed. Once placed into the position of power, with the altar beside it, no witch could pass. It was known.

Satisfied there were no threats to the caravan from wandering Whytes, Ciera left his position on the hillock and went to rejoin his people. "Ho there, Chara," he cried as he came into sight of the rear guard, letting them know he was no apparition.

"Ho there, Ciera," his friend responded. "It goes well?"

"It goes well, old friend. The will of our youth is strong, the strength of their arms carries us forward," he responded, looking with admiration at the team of youth stretching before him, each with the rope over their shoulder, dragging their great hope forward.

The huge wooden wheels creaked as the wagon master went back and forth dousing their axles with the thin oil used to help them turn. Chara came up on his horse, extending his palm upwards in greeting. "We will cover many miles today, Ciera. The ground is good, the path is clear, and the will of our young is strong."

"It is good, Chara," Ciera replied, holding his own palm up in salute. But he knew, come the end of the day, the treacherous road around the edge of the mountain must be surpassed. There was no other path for a heavy burden such as this, the marshlands were too soft for anything bar animals to cross. He knew, the Whytes would be waiting for them, the only denizens of the evil ones who could bear to live outside the mist. They could roll stones on their defenseless people, they could throw spears! But perhaps the tribe may be lucky and just have to battle the gradient. They would know soon enough.

His thoughts flew back to the old one.

Barely three months ago he had gone with tribute, a sacred relic had been found in one of the shattered homes of the ancient ones. Master Jack, as they knew him - Oh, how he had smiled, and then, the miracle! He connected a wire to the relic, and pressed its button - and from out of the depths of space, incredible music flowed.

"Irish folk songs," he had said. "A true gift my friend, a true gift indeed."

He was overjoyed that the Master was pleased. Just for this, his heart was full to overflowing, but to hear a miracle of the old age, that was a memory like as he would never have again. "It is beauty itself," he had said, in awe.

Master Jack smiled, "It is a miracle it survived. And as it turns, a day of miracles! The Theirn tribe has uncovered a relic, they have brought me images - may I show you?"

To so much as see the image of the holy relic filled him with awe, the great body, the arm reaching up, and the sheltering hand. He knew this to be the art of the Gods themselves, defying the weight of the sky, fighting back the forces of nature, the wild elements of chaos. He wept openly at the sight.

"To have the glories of the past revealed, it is a thing of beauty itself - but there is a task that has fallen to your tribe - As the gatherers of the ancient things, you have been gifted this by the Theirn, but for the reason of taking it from the cursed place and bringing it to where it will save our people. This monument is in the barren lands and must be fetched and taken to the edge of the green. It is a symbol of the old power, and placed at the perimeter will show the witches the greatest of our past and the threat of our present." Master Jack looked at the hardened warrior.

The Master of Horse for his tribe listened closely. Was the Master really gifting this task to his people? He nodded his acceptance of the words, yes, they would consider the great undertaking. But he felt a reticence.

"It is hard for you, Ciera, I know." the Master said softly. "To bear such an honor, to be the chosen, I understand you must think on this before you commit your tribe. But I ask it of you, and would bestow the great challenge on your brow, if you would accept it."

Ciera said little, it was difficult, to receive such an accolade as would be sung in sung for a thousand years. Was he worthy? He had faith in his tribe, they were strong, and for such an undertaking, many would come - to be part of history, to be part of the song. "I must go back to the elders," he said humbly, not willing or daring to snatch this glory for himself. "They must share the wisdom with us all, and do the choosing. I thank you for the offer, Master Jack, and am humbled by your faith in my people."

"As it must be, Ciera. Know the names of the two masterpieces - the one drawn, that is the Morin, but the other one, that goes with it, the altar you have NOT seen, that is the Morrigan."

Ciera gasped, "The Queen herself?" he said in astonishment.

"The Queen herself," nodded Master Jack, solemnly

The new people, the ones that emerged after the collapse, believed that the ancient mother could incarnate into certain sacred forms. If the Old Man said this was the Morrigan, surely her power could hold back the wraiths and the witches from the bleak lands - surely she had the power to withstand their evil magic.

Ciera had traveled with the witch hunters, deep into their world of desolation. The sun itself could not break through the curling darkness they draped over the lands they claimed - the earth died wherever they went. He knew without needing to speak to the others that they would, nay, they MUST undertake this sacred journey.

"The presence of the Morrigan has made the choice for us, Master Jack," he announced, making his commitment.

"Good, good - very good. I will arrange a sled and materials that you can use to move the monument. Speak to your tribe, bring as many able and willing souls as you can find. I will spread the word, you will have assistance from all in this most precious task."

The squeaking of the wheels brought him back to the present. It had been just two lunars since the journey began. Deep into the outlands they had gone, and there it was, the Morin. Beside it, the Morrigan herself, staring blankly back at them. He had not understood her silence, but the Master assured him, once she was in her place, her voice would come. Once more he was taken back to the past, where they retrieved the burden from the wastelands.

They had wound out the gantry, but the beast was heavy and would barely budge. Ciera solved the problem with his typical ingenuity, using the gantry with a lever, lifting the relic a bit at a time, and putting in stones to raise it higher. After a week they got it to the height of the wagon, itself a huge thing made of solid beams of wood with many wheels underneath. By lifting it enough to get in logs, they were then able to carefully roll the precious cargo onto the transportation, and tie the base of the Tor down, leaving its great arm to reach up and support the sky.

Once the earth was full of beasts who could pull such a thing, but in the savagery of the collapse, people fell onto the cows and all manner of edible animals, and now there were none. A few horses survived, such as those the leaders were granted, but not enough. No, this great burden was to be heaved along with the willing hearts of hundreds of the youth - and they did have hundreds!

Young men and women flocked from all the tribes to be part of the great journey of the Morrigan and the Morin. Thousands it grew to THOUSANDS, not hundreds. Every youth from every village answered the call! How could they not, this was history itself! It became such an issue just to feed them, that whole tribes committed to ferrying breads and oil to the caravan as it made its way to the edge of the fertile lands.

All knew this was a journey that had to happen. They had to stop the witches spreading, destroying their lands, ruining their crops. The Witch Hunters were fighting them back, but always another witch would come, more land would be twisted by their perversions. The youth knew their future depended on this task and drew the Tor on to its destiny.

Chara laughed, "Lost in dreams again, Ciera!"

The captain of the Quest was brought fully back, "The power of the Morrigan calls me," he explained. "She takes me on journeys, to the past, to the possible futures. The power of the mother is great."

"The power of the mother is good," replied his lieutenant.

ooo0000ooo

"The Morin and the Morrigan? Are you serious?" Cliff Trilby had come to the archaeologist who acted as a trader, collecting the rare items of old earth so prized by his folk, plus gathering the necessary fresh foods for the station while delivering the important tools and necessities to the locals. "But I guess a high-frequency transmitter will work. The witches hate random signals like that, disturbs their song."

Master Jack, known as Professor Jack Blake to his off-world friends, smiled, "With these people, you have to couch things in terms of reverence and symbol. They may be primitive, but they are incredibly brave. With nothing but their wits, they go out and fight the menace that circulates their world. But while I direct them, I cannot be seen to be doing it directly, so I use the old language and the concept of the quest to motivate them to defend their borders. They truly live in fear of the Ethereals, you know."

Cliff Trilby was a descendant of the mining missions that had returned to this ruined planet. "It is a disturbing occurrence. I am no psyche-analyst but what I gather is that there is a sort of breach between dimensions happening. When they used no-matter bombs it destabilized the lines between the natural forces, and so this witch thing happens. It is only on this continent, thank God."

Trader Jack, as he was commonly known, was fairly severe in his response, "It is a harsh world out there, but the locals are making it work. I think they could do with a little bit of help from you lot. For one, you don't know if the blight will stay isolated here. Yes, I know this was the only place that the new weapons got used, but we don't know where other channels might open up."

Cliff shook his head, "Jack, no one knows - The world as we knew it ended a hundred and thirty years ago. But you know we can't come in - it would ruin their fragile society. These people are not capable of understanding technology, they WORSHIP it for god's sake. You know this has been resolved - If we turn up in our anti-gravs we will become their gods, and disturb their evolution. Non-interference is working, they are growing, finding their way, and you are helping them. But I have to ask - why the huge broken corner of a skyscraper? Sure, give them the frequency transmitter, makes perfect sense, not so difficult to transport - but carting a huge block of concrete two hundred miles? That is just insane! Especially as it will do absolutely nothing against the Witches."

"Here you are dead wrong, that useless lump of concrete will do everything. Not for what it is, but for what it represents. They call it 'The Tor' you know and while it is nothing, because of the massive coordinated effort needed to shift it cross country to the perimeter, the entire nation of tribes has been forced to work together. All their young are there, hauling it along with the transmitter to the coordinates I gave them. Cliff, BECAUSE they have something to believe, BECAUSE it is difficult to achieve, this is what gives them strength, purpose, and focus."

He leaned back, pulled some herb from his pouch and packed a pipe. "Catnip?" he asked his visitor.

"You got some of that brandy they make here?" asked Cliff in return.

As they sat looking out from the top floor of the hydroelectric station, all glass, gazing over the vast plains below and huge lake behind, the weed and the alcohol took hold, and the two friends started laughing, telling stories of the old days. Finally, Cliff broached the taboo. "Jack, you have been recalled to Canter. I argued against it, saying you were making valuable discoveries, that your archaeological work was still essential, but there are old heads saying this is already too much - they are worried you will let slip something of what lies over the ocean. They are saying they want you back to discuss terms of engagement, but we both know what will happen once you leave."

"Cliff, old friend, this is my home now. I love these people, simple, honest, hard-working. They have nothing, yet they have everything. Canter City is an empty drum, beating out its self-importance. It has little meaning to me, other than as a supplier of conveniences. I have a ninety-year history here, if that is not enough to convince petty bureaucrats that I am not a risk to their precious notion of non-integration, then nothing I say there will change their minds. And what are they going to do? Come here and arrest me? What will be the charges? Following the charter?"

"I know - Believe me I know. It is the academics demanding you leave, the politicians are on the fence, some saying you have been here long enough, others saying it is a point of connection to the old country, a sort of ambassadorship. As you say, you have been here over ninety years, but BECAUSE of this there are a lot of people who think you are due to retire." Cliff sipped a little more of the brandy.

"The term *'due to retire'* is best understood as *'I want that nice fat posting'*, yes?" They both knew the power station was a place of significance. Any who held it engendered respect, but more importantly, it could be worked to earn a smart operator a fortune. They were essentially jealous, imagining Jack Blake was making vast profits.

"You know the standing joke? Your trading post is called "The Embassy" by the kids. They love it and want to come here, feel the thrill of the wild lands, and all that. This is what is really worrying the old heads back home who want to keep you in check, because they know that when you are gone, this place will become a doorway for adventurers. It is a fair consideration. On the other foot, it IS some ninety-four years, and the word is they really want someone new and fresh out here." Cliff didn't want to take his friend back to civilization and knew full well what a disturbance in the fabric of this society it would make for their trader to vanish.

"New and fresh? Obedient, you mean. It's all horse crap, Cliff. The locals accept me, and the stuff they find is not only useful back home, it gives me a chance to feed in seeds and things that they need for their survival. As far as kids joyriding out here, that's not my concern, nor my problem. Here, did you see what was found the other month?" Jack pulls out the recorder Ciera had discovered, and plugged it in, letting the sweet Irish melodies flow out around the eagle nest.

"Far out, Jack. A recorder? Still functioning despite war and disaster. That is amazing!"

"The past IS amazing my old friend. The past also needs respecting. Cliff, you are all born of mining stock, descended from miners, so understand this - The past is what I mine. This is my world and I want no other. They talk about non-interference? Well, they can try practicing it and just leave me alone. I don't need their pretentious guidelines to tell me to tread carefully with these people, I have been doing it most of my life," he snorted his disgust at the stupidity.

"Believe me, I am on your side! Given my druthers, I would let the sleeping dog lie but I am told I have to bring you back, for review they say. I don't want to do this, you don't want to go, but it is past a decade since your last visit to home base and now they are insisting. I can't force you, I won't force you, but the next ship they send won't have me on board, but security personnel who will just drag you out of here."

Jack laughed, "Come in guns a-blazing, hey? To do what? Arrest a man for doing his job? We both know what will happen if I go back, an endless round of panels and discussions and round tables about the fate of the new nations, how we can best serve, yadda yadda yadda. After all this time the fools still cannot see how much they have already interfered, just by providing hoes and seed. Interference was never the problem, correct guidance is what was, and still is, needed."

Cliff smiled, his old friend was long in the tooth and set in his ways, but he was right. The Federation of Mining Engineers was originally a trade union, set up to protect miners' rights. They had no business nor any authority to govern, yet they had assumed the mantle as there was no one else. The desolation the Canter had returned to after its twenty-year tour was absolute - cities shattered, the population dead, and a deadly ionic cloud that reflected the sunlight, putting the land under a constant shadow where barely anything grew.

When the scavenger bots were done, the atmospheric ions were stabilized and sunlight once more flowed over the land, but it had mutated. Things had changed far more than what was possible inside twenty years, which was when they realized, the ship must have grooved into a gravity well and flowed forward on the timeline - their twenty-odd years was more like three hundred for those on the planet.

It was no longer their place of origin. There were still people, primitive cave dwellers, but also the awful abomination of the witches - once human creatures, that had adapted to sucking off energy from people and the land. Like the classical vampires of legend, these creatures absorbed energy, not blood, but the effect was the same. Once they got their hooks into a human, all that was left was a shell, a ghost of sorts - still living, but better off dead.

These were the Whytes, pale-skinned creatures that did the bidding of their mistress. They were able to venture into moonlight, grabbing children and old folk who strayed too near the boundary, taking them back to feed their Witch. The league of miners realized the people needed help, but the humans that survived were little more than apes who were scared of the flying craft that came. The miners needed fresh food and had thought they could teach these primitives to grow what they needed. They tried to teach them how to use tools, develop agriculture, and procure the other things that the Canter needed, like fruit and vegetables, but the people were too scared.

This was the rub, the lands across the water from the London base of the Canter were fertile and populated - So the consortium thrown together to manage the planet determined that they should train the locals to be farmers, thus ensuring their food supply. Except they were miners, with no people skills at all.

This was when Jack Blake came up with his plan: set up trade with the locals, exchange things for what they need - for seed, for hoes, for water rights. Ease into a transition. Once they were self-sufficient in food they could move along the path to civilization once more. Without waiting for the arguments to run their course, he came out here and established his base in an old hydroelectric station - a place that had somehow survived the change and which still had a dam that held water. The generators were no longer functional, this world had ceased to use grid power centuries ago, but the channels for the water could be directed towards irrigation.

"We need to fast track people from the caves and hunter-gathering into an agricultural society," that was Jack's proposal and as a Professor of Antiquities, brought along as part of a then government requirement on every long-range mining vessel for potential discoveries on the outer rim, he was ideally placed and qualified. "Fair trade is no man's loss!" he had declared to the assembly, and eventually they voted him the right to establish his outpost. What was it, ninety-four years ago now?

"What are the chances they will let me back?" Jack asked, feeling resigned to his fate.

"No chance with the academics, twenty percent with the politicians, and not one of the miners want you about - they want to get in here and start digging," Cliff answered earnestly.

"Cliff, truth is, I only have five to ten years left. I may live a little longer with access to medical assistance at the station, your glorified floating city, but the angels are calling. Take back a proposal, tell them I am sick and old and not up for the rigor of scientific questioning and extended consultations. Instead, suggest that they send a replacement that I can train up. I will need a student of antiquities, one well versed in ancient agricultural practices. Bring them back on your next trip, and I will spend a few years teaching them the ropes."

Cliff inclined his head, "That is a fairly major concession. The Academics might go for it, getting one of their own in here has been a long term goal. Once they sign off on the notion, the politicians will be swayed, and the mining consortium still has plenty of unpopulated lands to hunt in - for what, I have no idea."

"Addiction, Cliff. It is what they do, despite the fact they have no market to sell to they still want the precious metals, the gold, silver, and platinum. The excuse is refinement and repair of electronics, but really, they just want to show off their robot wives loaded up with pretty things. They don't run things, however. So get this proposal through and we can continue our regular pipes. More catnip?"

"Don't mind if I do - it is vastly better than the hydro they grow at the station. And another wee dram, if you could be so kind!"

Jack laughed, they had made a good team for decades and would do so for a few more years. Canter City engineered the grow pods that resurrected the ancient grains, and research crews found the seed banks stored centuries ago, which meant that with a little DNA engineering they could recreate the various fruits and vegetables that once grew in abundance. This, allied to the water from the dam behind them, is what allowed the locals to emerge from the caves.

As they puffed the weed and felt the mellow softness roll over their thoughts, Jack loosened up from the tension. "The real trick, Cliff my lad, is to look like we haven't chosen a specific candidate, and that the academics have picked the one THEY want. I think we will need a team of four prospects. We can put them to tests in the field, that sort of thing. I can design it that only the right one will WANT to stay. If it is not MY decision, but a case of the last person standing, they will not object."

"I have been doing this run for thirty years now, Jack. My father did the run for almost sixty before this. I never knew who was the first, or how you got started. How did you build the trust in the tribes that got all this going?" Cliff was curious.

"Ah, well, people may appear to change, but they don't. The secret was that Patrick O'Shea and myself understood human nature. Paddy was the first to do the run you know ."

"The war pilot? I never knew that."

"Neither of us fitted in with the station. His death is what taught us about the dangers of this place, a sad and early demise. Anyway, enough of melancholy, what we did was trickery. We approached no one, offered nothing, kept completely to ourselves. We laid down pipe, we leveled fields, we dug by hand the trenches to plant the trees and the grains.

"By sprouting saplings, and transferring them to the field with regular water, we were getting fruits inside a few years. Grains the first year, of course, and the baking of these drew the locals in. They did not trust strangers of course, but their hunger brought them closer. We saw them staring, and indicated with sign language that we would swap a loaf of bread for a spear, that sort of thing. We didn't need the spear, but it was a thing they valued, and so the bread became a thing of worth," he laughed at the simplicity of it.

"When Queen Elizabeth the First succeeded to the throne, the potato had been discovered and brought back to Britain. The thing is, no one wanted it - a strange vegetable that grew underground - it was the devil's fruit. But James who succeeded her saw the potential, and instead of trying to foist the new vegetable on the people, he did the opposite. He built a secret garden and insisted it be kept only for himself and the royal household. Soon enough, his subjects were stealing his potatoes and growing them in their own gardens. We did the same.

"We made everything expensive, so expensive that the locals stole grain, stole fruits, and planted their own. Now they needed information, so instead of us offering to teach, they came and offered skins, things in exchange for the knowledge they needed. It took a decade, but we built up trust and faith, and more importantly, we developed lines of communication with tribal chiefs and elders. Once they acknowledged us, the rest just followed suit."

"What happened to Patrick? They say he got caught by a witch."

"Aye laddy, he was. But you didn't hear anything of the whole story." Jack puffed once more on his freshly packed pipe, offering more herb to his friend. "Because of the non-interference thing, we could not let it out, but Patrick was the one who was the original Witch Hunter. He was the one who trained the village boys how to catch them, how to use the ionic nets. And of course, where do you think the idea of using a coin to entrance them came from? We eventually minted our own coins, gold, silver, and bronze. But back then, we used old Earth ones into which we placed resonance filters.

"I can't tell you the excitement we felt when we caught our first one. To see the clouds roll back and the land become free, it was a glorious sight. Of course, none of it made its way into any report - the locals just discovered a way to reclaim land from the abominations. The only role WE played was in showing them how to use the ionic nets, and how to weave them from the alloys. Patrick loved his work, he was never happier."

"So a witch finally got him?" Cliff was enthralled. Of course, he could never tell anyone about this, not while Jack lived, but what a tale.

"Not just any witch, the head bitch. We had no idea they had a hierarchy, only that some witches were stronger than others. But one day, the call went out, and Patrick with his usual joy of hunting got together a crew - a HUGE disturbance was pushing the mist forward, crouching over lands we had settled with villages and crops. He went in, and by the report of the one young apprentice that survived, he netted her - but it didn't work like it did with the others - she USED the net to draw him in. Then she took him over, made him her slave. But not for long - His apprentice netted and killed her while she was distracted, but she got to Paddy and killed him before she died. A sad end to a great man. "

"How many other secrets have been buried out here?" Cliff was fascinated, just like a witch was when you rolled a coin in front of her.

"How often have we broken protocol and interfered, you mean?" laughed Jack. "Lots of instances, Cliff my lad. But every one of them necessary. If we had not taught them how to trap a witch, all these lands would have already been overrun, no food would go back to the station, and you would all be back to living on synthetics. I have bent and twisted every rule out here - It is why I had to be on my own. But now, it is a time to share, to teach another the path, so that these pure souls can continue."

"It was never about feeding the station for you, was it?" Cliff smiled, understanding at last what drove this man's solitary existence.

"It was all about tending to the flock, being the good shepherd, and guarding them from the wolves. Of course, they expect to be shorn once a year while the station must get its due, that is just fair trade. But no, my real reason is to watch these remarkable creatures grow and flourish, and for the most part, it is standing back, offering advice. But occasionally, like later today, we must go and set up the resonance machine out there at the edge of the territory." Jack looked at Cliff, waiting for him to offer.

He laughed, "So we need to cloak and fly you out there. Can I stay and watch?"

"Indeed, that would be a fair trade." Jack was smiling. Cliff made a good accomplice.

The Last Leg

Ciera knew in his bones that the Queen had attracted jealous suitors. "I can feel them, Chara. The Whytes are here, we cannot risk the journey without securing the road. We need to send spearman up that slope, and slingers as well. It would be a great dishonor to lose any of the tribes to the witches at this late hour."

"Why would the Queen allow it?" Chara was confused. Surely this journey, this exhausting effort, was all to ensure the presence of the Morrigan would repel the evil ones. While they had it, surely none could approach.

"She sleeps, Chara. I am to meet Master Jack at the designated place, only then will he provide the keys to awaken the blessed one," he explained. Chara seemed doubtful. This too is the way of things, that last inch is longer than the first mile. But Ciera had no doubts, or if he did they were diffused by the confidence he had in Master Jack.

Yet he had learned, best to have questions out in the open. This was the way, one might doubt, but one can resist it with a reasoned view of why it is so. "Do you doubt Master Jack's word, Chara? I can understand if this may be so - It is a difficult journey, our nerves are frayed, our patience tested. But consider this - When has Master Jack ever failed us?

"Surely, I can doubt if clouds will come tomorrow when I look at the blue sky. I can see no evidence of a cloud before me, so why should I believe? But the cycles have shown us, clouds will come, if not tomorrow, then the day after, or the day after that. Our belief in the cloud is not in question, just as I understand that your belief in the Queen is not in question, am I right?"

His most ardent supporter for the journey, the one who stood up to the elders when they accused Ciera of avarice, of wanting all the glory, was less resolute. "I do not know the Master like yourself, Ciera. I am sure he speaks his truth, but now we are almost there I cannot see him. Has he wings to fly? There is no one following us on this road."

"Well, this is truth. My answer is, I do not know. But just as I know the clouds will come and the rain will fall, I know Master Jack has always been here for us. Always. Providing us with not just tools and seed, but with wisdom. He is one who knows, Chara, even when we do not. What I believe, what I know, is that change will come. Doubts are not wrong, they can assist the change. It is right to doubt - just as I presently doubt we will have an easy pass over this rise. But it is not an unreasonable doubt. If you are going to attack the caravan, this is the place.

"It is not wrong to doubt, but it is wise to understand where they come from. Perhaps your doubts are an echo of a deeper intuition, my friend. I do believe we will soon battle the Whytes. But, let us worry about tomorrow when it comes - for now, pass the word along, prepare the youth with weapons and bring out the chocks to stop the Tor rolling out of control."

Chara nodded, "Perhaps you are right Ciera. The uncertainty in my heart may be a truth of a different kind, a sensing of danger. We know the witches paralyze their victims with fear, fill their heads with doubts. Perhaps what I feel is a sending, a warning."

"Everything is a test, we pass or we fail. Yet in this test we cannot dream of failure, we cannot let it enter our thoughts. This is the great journey, the accomplishment of our generation, and we two are the proud bearers of our tribe." Ciera spoke his words of encouragement, then nodded to his deputy to be on his business, preparing the youth for what will come.

"And Chara, if the Whytes do come, there will be multitudes. More than we have ever seen. The witches will want to stop this progress and they will throw all their will to this. And why? Because they know the importance of this quest. They know we will be erecting a barrier against their incursions and they will seek to break our spirit and scatter our people. Expect difficulty in the next hours, find courage in your heart, and share it with the others so they remain steadfast."

The barren hillside before them did not look as if it could hide so much as a hare. It was rocks and dust, rising from the plains to a plateau. They would be pulling the Tor up a gradient for some thirty miles, and before the end, tiredness and exhaustion would begin to weaken their spirits. It would be easy to roll stones down on the company, and then try and roll the trailer, as it was very top-heavy. If it fell over here, sliding down to the soft soil below, they may never recover it.

Prayers to the Gods do not help adjust gravity, he had noted. Their fate lay in the slow and certain progress through this region. As it was, the noon day sun was fast approaching. It was time for lunch, for rest, and to make the hard journey in the hours closer to dark. Here on the flat, there was little risk of attack. He blew the horn, calling for the rest period, and watched with satisfaction as the kitchen staff arrived with water and bread and oil for all.

The conversation was pleasant, the youth were tired but still willing. The bread and oil were taken with cheese and dried tomato, along with some watered wine. The Shade cloths were draped off the Tor, reaching out to provide shade from the noon sun. Ciera listened with half an ear to the chatter but his mind was on that hill - not particularly high. They had raised the Tor over steeper inclines, but the land here was dry and dusty, easy for a sandal to slip.

The road was in good repair, not flagged, but a hard, firm dirt that would not sink. Then it struck him, all the Whytes need do is to create a weakness in the shoulder - a road that felt firm underfoot could have a softness dug in below it, and all it would take was a small sideways movement for the whole thing to come crashing down.

Scouts were always out, with bow and arrow, not just hunting game, but watching for movement, seeing if the enemy were close. Nothing had been reported, no smoke raised, no call echoed off the boulders. Why did he feel this certainty? It was as if the Queen had spoken to his heart, could he deny it? And how could you test such a thing?

He called over the wagon master, who was taking the respite from constant movement to check the strutting and ties, ensuring the wagon was in good order. "Ho Maiche, how goes the cart?"

"Ho Ciera, it is well as can be expected after such a journey. Surely it has suffered, we have some cracked bowsprits, some of the timbers holding the Tor have begun to fracture, but it will suffice to complete the journey." The wagon master was pleased to report.

"Tell me, Master of Wagons, if you were to attack this caravan, with a thousand and more hands to defend it, would you not imagine the best assault would be to weaken the shoulder of the road at a critical juncture - create a softness that would cause her to tip down the soft soils below us?"

The Wagon master considered the question, "Aye," he replied. "That is the very thing a cunning and deceitful creature like a witch would do."

"Then how can we test this road we are about to travel? We can choose corners, areas most likely to be vulnerable, and inspect them, but how can we know if the ground is firm enough to take out quest?" Ciera had some knowledge of flagging a road in a village, but as to securing foundations, all he knew was that when an area failed, water had gotten under and taken out the substratum. "We have all seen a road sink and can easily spot where such a thing needs work, but if the witches were cunning they would create a surface that looked solid, but which was not, would you agree?"

Maiche agreed, "How do you know if the apple is rotten at the core unless you bite it? Perhaps the witches have cursed a vulnerable spot, what you suggest is concerning Ciera. I have no suggestion to counter this possibility, I am no engineer."

"Without causing panic, could you spend this lunch speaking to the youth, seeing if any have knowledge of such things? If it comes from yourself, there will be no questions raised, you are simply seeking to ensure the safety of the wagon."

"It will be so, Ciera. Any wisdom to be found shall be found." Maiche assented to the task.

"My father used to say holes formed when some underground spring bubbled up, but out here, and on a hill like this, who could say. Look for a patch of green and down the hill from there water could make its way." A girl whose father was a builder in a R'arch clan had good advice.

But the most sensible came from the son of a blacksmith. "Anything solid rings to the tune of its making," the boy said. "Metal, wood, earth, they sing a different song, but when you beat the road with a large hammer, you will hear when it changes composition. This is known."

Ciera had ordered a conclave and a halt to the caravan, the first in some two lunars. There had been murmurs of concern, but living and working with such a diverse group of interests had galvanized the political heart of the leading group. Chara, as his right hand, had brought the gavel down, bringing the meeting to order. "Here ye, the conclave of wisdom is called for the progression of the great Tor to its destination at the edge of the green."

One by one, Ciera had interested parties speak their piece, each holding the stone of truth. It was the wise suggestion by his mother that he brought the tribal crystal, for it had been used on several occasions in committing the energy of those present to a singular focus. He had learned much of statesmanship on this journey. The importance of recognizing every soul, listening to their needs, patiently explaining your course, all these things he had learned.

As a hunter of the ancient paths, he had little interest in the machinations of power, but given this task, he had come to understand that the ways of his elders were wise. But if the truth be known, it was his mother who had advised him on how to proceed, just as she had advised his father, may he rest in slumber.

Many voices spoke, of how this was needed, or that. But the predominant agreement was the need to complete the task before the harvest season was upon them, as the youth would be needed back at the family farms. At this point, Ciera finally arose to speak. He held out his hand, and the speaker of the conclave took the stone from the last member and handed it to him. All would be silent while he spoke his truth. "I have but one question. If the harvest season started tomorrow, would you tell your people to return to their villages, to perhaps come back here in a few months to complete the task?"

The was a general muttering, and a few hands rose to offer a response. "The stone sees Marth of Thiern tribe. Will you speak?"

He was a father of three, a head man of his tribe, the one that discovered the artifact. "I would speak for my people. We could survive a harvest with only the old men and the women bringing in the grains. We cannot survive the witches coming into our lands. Yes, I know they are far from where we live, but all I can say is that I hold dear this sacred task. Nothing and no one must be allowed to alter its course."

He sat down to a general murmur of assent. "Are there any who dispute this wisdom from the one who discovered the Tor?" asked Ciera. A muttering, a few strained faces. To be expected. "It has been long, it has been arduous, but it is agreed by this conclave that we must not falter. All stamp your foot three times if you agree!"

All stamp their right foot. "Are there any who wish to naysay?"

There are no voices raised. Ciera smiled, he knew this was the only likely result, but the people needed to hear it for themselves. Air the grievances, listen to the song of sadness, and make it sweet with logic. This he had learned. "However, I have a concern. The Queen has spoken to my heart, warning me the witches will not let us place our burden down easily. From what quarter, in what way, I have not been told. But we have had the wagon master go forth, speaking with the youth, asking about potential issues, and we have some answers. This conclave must now come to agreement as to the best way forward."

The Wagon master stood and explained the issues. Should the road have been weakened, the catastrophic consequence that could then follow. Should the caravan be assaulted, and the likely way this might occur. Then the suggestion of finding a spring and beating the road ahead to test for hardness was offered as a sure way forward. All agreed.

"Then this evening we rest. Tomorrow we begin the great task, the last stage of this journey, crossing the mountain and reaching the plateau upon which our burden shall be laid down and the Queen consecrated." All left with no objections. It was a good plan.

Chara stayed behind. "Scouts reveal no spring, no Whytes. The road to the plateau is but thirty miles of incline, and once there the ground is firm. With luck, no more than two days, Ciera - Two days!" he was visibly moved.

"The Gods have smiled on us, Chara. Let us pray to the moon and the stars this evening, but let us also erect barricades and place guards. If the Whytes will fall on us, this is the place, this is the time. Tell each camp to have weapons at the ready. All being well, at dawn we begin the assault on the mountain."

Ciera prayed to the moon that night, she was full and sweet, blessing him with her guidance. But it also gave light to those who would attack them, for the Whytes were so pale they were next to invisible on such an evening. Of course, they had brought dogs with them for this purpose, for no matter how stealthy a creature might be, they cannot hide their scent. Whytes were not fighters, they were creatures of cunning. They would creep out on such a night to steal a human for their overlord, but Ciera felt in his bones there was a greater threat. With luck, the ones he had sent for last week would arrive on the morrow.

The engineering solution to the strength of the road seemed sound, he had tested it himself, tapping the various types of ground. The road gave a sort of ring to the hammer, where soft soil gave none. It was as good a test as they could hope for. The search for a spring was a good idea - not just for the road - but because setting up a water station here could only be a good thing.

But then a dog howls. "Oh no, no no no." Ciera exclaims as he pulls a horn and blows it sharply, three times. An attack warning. The only thing approaching the camp of men will be things not afraid of humans, and out here, that could only be Whytes. "To arms!" he shouts. "Gather torches, surround the Tor!"

There is a flash on his right, Ciera already has his sword out and was striking in its direction - the metal bites the thin flesh of a Whyte, it squeals. Dammit, they knew to come straight for him? "All up, Whytes are attacking, gather round the Tor!" he shouts again.

Chara is there, "Your wisdom astounds me, Ciera." He carries a flaming pot and arrows, dipping them in as he comes towards where his Captain stood. "If we had been on the road, stretched to a narrow phalanx with all those rocks for Whytes to hide behind, we would have had no chance. Here they must come across open fields, and the opposite is true."

The warriors are already with him, forming up a flank in front of the Tor. Torches were being lit, braziers were aflame, and now with the red glow of the fire, the Whytes become more easily seen. There are thousands of them, hobbling their strange running gait as they pour down the road.

"Oil! Bring up the oil! Archers, to your post. We know what must be done, and by the Gods, we will do it!!" shouted Ciera. It was known that the witches would put up resistance, which is why this last leg had a military unit come - but they were far from the mist, and the holy light of fire weakens the hold of the witches over these ghosts.

Archers climb aboard the wagon, lighting their special arrows in the flame pots, and launching volley after volley at the approaching hoard. The Whytes ignite once the flame touches their skin, and the splash of flame from the landing arrows lights up other Whytes around them. "Archers, light, aim, FIRE! Light! Aim! FIRE!" Chara is shouting with a fierce intensity, willing the men through their fear.

All knew what happened if a Whyte dragged you off, you were taken back to the witch and made her slave. No free man could bear such a thought. "Light, Aim, FIRE?" Chara shouted. More and more fell, but they kept coming.

Ciera took a flange of spearmen, the tips of the javelins similarly lit by fire. "Forward men, defend the Tor. Slaughter these creatures!" Now the youth had come to wakefulness, and though confused, they understood what must be done. They grabbed a hold of anything that burned and formed a barrier between the creatures and the Tor.

Thousands of Whytes fell, thousands more came to take their place. Fire launched through the skies, swords slashed and cut, even the youth had taken weapons and were shouting their father's names as they attacked the interlopers. Ciera was proud - they stood to fight for the Gods, for the journey, and for the good of all men. They would risk their own lives to ensure others had a future.

The tide seemed to be thinning, with the odd one breaking through the ranks, only to end on a spear or at the edge of a sword. They were not fighters, these Whytes, just driven shells of what were once men. Even so, their sheer numbers would have overwhelmed the quest if they had not had encampments up and oil pots ready - it seemed that they would win this night.

Then a howl came up from the archers, behind them a huge figure came up from the meadow, a giant of a thing, the size of ten men. "Turn and fire!" Chara ordered his men, but while the arrows pierced, the fire did not ignite this thing. It seemed a dank green color, as best as Ciera could tell, some sort of swamp creature.

"Spear, turn and charge that thing - keep it from the Tor." Ciera could guess at its plan, to pull the relic over, trying to smash it. On one hand, he felt a grim satisfaction that the witches knew what harm this could do to them and would create a creature capable of attacking it. On the other, a terrible fear that it might succeed.

Volley after volley of spear sailed through the night sky, the lit heads of the shafts forming a flaming arc, hitting the beast, causing it pain as it howled. It was a dance of fire, arching up, then down, embedding itself into the evil magic, seeking to purify the land of the poison. But it did not stop the thing. It must have been bred with a skin both resistant to fire, and very thick. "Aim for its eyes!" he ordered the archers. *Blind it, see how well it copes then.*

It screams as several found their mark, but still it raged on. Chara drew some archers back from the front, "Maintain fire on the Whytes!" he shouted, for they were still coming. But nothing would stop the monster, it started to run at the Tor and Ciera feared it would smash into it, a suicide mission to break the charm and prevent the quest from succeeding. As it barraged close he could see it clearly, one eye blind, another barely open as it held up an arm to protect it. It was an ugly deformed head atop a massive torso. The thing would have been the match of a hundred men, but it fired no weapon, swung no cudgel - Instead it reached the wagon, and then did what he had never imagined.

The beast reached down where the Morrigan had been tied and covered with canvas, and it ripped it upwards. It tore through the very ropes, causing the wagon to shake, but succeeded in tearing it from its podium. Ciera felt despair, deep, dark despair. It was going for the Queen herself! The monster now had its prize, and it ran, it ran from the flaming arrows and spears, and there was nothing they could do to stop it.

When it turned, so did the last of the Whytes, scattering back to the darkness, but what did it matter - the Morrigan was taken. A collective howl went up through the tribes as each began to grasp what had happened. Grief struck Ciera in the heart, as surely as the spears and arrows struck down the Whytes, he fell to his knees in despair. How could the Queen have allowed it? What had they done wrong that opened the door for this evil?

Chara shook him to his sense. "Ciera, to me! We must pursue that thing, hunt it down! It has the Morrigan!"

The blackness lifted with the courage of his officer. He fought back the despair, forced down the truth that even if they caught the monster, what could they do? The truth was if they DIDN'T act, they would forever curse themselves. "You are right my friend." Then he turned to the troupe, blowing his horn for silence.

There was still weeping, and tears, but enough could hear his voice now. "We must hunt that creature, bring it down. I know not how we will do this, but we must. Tomorrow, you all know what you must do. You all know your part - the Tor must continue on its journey. Somehow, we will find that beast and bring back the Morrigan. For now, I will take a team with horses and we will ride after it!"

It was at that point that salvation came clopping up the road behind them, a team of horses from which a voice of silent power almost whispered, "Seems we are a little late to the party. Did someone mention hunting a monster?"

Ciera wheeled round, by the great Gods of mercy, the Witch Hunters had finally arrived!

Hunting the Queen

Cliff Trilby had his hands on the trigger, ready to disobey the non-interference directive, when Jack reached over to stay his hand, saying, "Let this play out."

He looked in astonishment, "I would have thought this is exactly where you bent the rules. You can't give the witches a frequency generator - if they learn how to work it, they will take over the whole damn place."

Jack shook his head. "You need to trust these people. They are incredibly resourceful, but I am glad you are starting to see the light. That is US down there, without the benefit of education of technology. There but for the grace of God, and all that. Even so, we have to let them lift the burden and bear the brunt of the task, otherwise, they will never grow."

"I am not disagreeing with you, Jack - you know these folk better than anyone alive, but it seems to me that these witches are much smarter than we gave credit for. Just understanding that thing was a threat to them, for one, tells us that whatever is in that mist is intelligent, resourceful, and a real danger. They managed to recognize the problem before it arrived, develop a tactic to remove it, and successfully implement the plan. But more importantly, the question: Where the hell did they get a giant from?"

For a long moment, Jack said nothing. "Cliff, what we are seeing is an entire evolution of a species, not just our people, but the witches as well. They are a unique race, of unknown origin, though the old myths contain elements of what they are. I consider it entirely possible that the use of the No Matter bombs caused a rift between dimensions, and opened our planet up to an alternative reality."

Cliff sat back, considering the notion. "Well, sure, such a thing has been suggested. But there are other possibilities. For one, maybe we shifted ourselves into a different dimension when we gravity hooked the event horizon getting back here. Maybe we didn't just shift in time, but in space as well. But we aren't quantum physicists and we don't even have tools for measuring such a thing, let alone doing the math."

Jack smiled, "But we learn. That is what we do as a race, we face an obstacle and we learn to negotiate it. As an example, as a professor of archaeology, I had to learn a whole batch of cross-referenced skills, language being one of them. Those people speak Arabic, Cliff. Do you know the odds of us crossing to a different dimension, meeting a people who look and act like us, and who also speak the same language from our original world?"

"Let me guess, next to impossible?"

"As you say, next to impossible. Plus, we have the same cities and monuments, albeit in ruins, yet we are missing one - just ONE - of the ancient wonders. Now, this IS entirely impossible, it just can't happen. It is either the planet we left, or it isn't." Jack looks at his pilot.

"The Pyramids, yeah, that is hell strange. No one can explain that."

Jack laughs, "Your people are miners, Cliff. They don't care to think about anything other than the best way to get to a seam. But I do care. We know WHY they are missing, they got hit by No-Matter bombs, but this led me to ask WHY they were built in the first place. You know the dates given for their building have been dis-proven? Geological water wear on the sphinx showed over 6000 years of rain. Given the Sahara turned to desert around 5,000 BCE in the old scale, then the Sphinx could not have been built after 11,000 BCE.

"Now IT is still here - but Cliff, there are no pyramids beside it. In this world, it almost seems they were never built."

"So, ah, this why you wanted the resonance machine put beside the Sphinx?" the light was dawning in his eyes.

"This is EXACTLY why we are putting it beside the Sphinx. What I think, what I suspect at least, is that the ancient culture was shown, or had a dream, or something that said they needed a huge energy to stop the mist. It had to be big, to get an entire culture creating such massive monoliths. Hell, maybe even miners from space turned up and told them to create huge resonance chambers. However it played out, have you considered the pyramids were built BECAUSE they needed to generate a frequency to keep the door shut to whatever dimension was seeping through." Jack waited for Cliff to soak up what he was really saying.

Cliff just shook his head, "Man, that is one huge concept right there. But all the more reason to stop that Giant getting the resonance machine back to the witches. I still have it targeted - we can do this and all that will happen is the locals will find a dead giant with the Morrigan, as you call it, lying there. No one will know it was us!"

It was tempting, make everything clean and simple, but no matter that it would not be seen, it was still chopping off a vital stage of growth for his people. Jack just said, "We let it play out. Only as a last resort do we step in. How long before it reaches the blighted lands?"

Cliff did a few calculations, "Well, seems that the locals did do a lot of damage, the damn thing is limping badly, and seems confused - it is not making a direct line back home. Wonder what that is about?"

"Might be the generator. Even though it is not on, the interaction between its base frequency and that thing will be polarized opposites. This is the thing, the witches operate on frequency - maybe in THEIR world, what we see as grey death, they see as green and living. Maybe it is like how insects see things on a completely different wavelength to us and experience a different world. Where is it headed?"

Cliff laughs, "You gonna love this, on the current zig-zag, it may even end up at the sphinx! Damn, wouldn't that be strange?"

"Let go and trust - it is a basic understanding of these people. Something we could all learn to practice. Have the Witch Hunters turned up at the quest camp yet?"

"Yeah yeah, your favorite boy and his posse are there." Cliff adjusts the scope, "And, as you predicted, they are making their way out over the flats, following the giant."

"Cliff, tell me the one astounding things about those flats, as you call them. What is the other great change?"

"What, you mean the Sahara is now a paradise of green? Yeah, the climate change really worked in its favor."

Jack just nodded. Another thing out of place and out of time. "Stay up and keep tracking the beast. If it starts to find its way back to the mist, put a couple of shots at its feet, and send it back to Giza. Drop me down close to the Witch Hunters, I will take a hover bike to say hello. All going well I will meet you at the Sphinx. Don't kill it unless you absolutely have to, our boys have the ability to bring that thing down, and they need the legends if they are going to build a new society."

ooo0000ooo

Ciera was overjoyed, the great one himself was here, "Master Artrim, welcome to our camp. You are most needed, a monster has come and taken the Morrigan. We have to catch it, slay it, and save the Queen!"

Pherial Artrim looked at the bitter battle that had ensued, the many thousands of Whytes dead, clearly visible in the moonlight now their life had left them. It was a curious thing, Master Jack had given him special glasses, not just for glare, but to tell the difference between the living and the dead. Polarized light, he had called it. If you saw a living Whyte with your natural eyes, it seemed almost ghost-like, especially in moonlight, its natural home. Once you killed them, that illusionary light left, so he imagined they had a Soul of sorts. But wearing the glasses, even when in their mockery of living they came up as grey, dead creatures, motivated by spite and scorn.

"A fine battle, Master Ciera. You achieved much, I have never seen so many Whytes dead in one place. It is worthy of song." he said in that calm, commanding voice.

"We achieved nothing," Ciera cried. "They gained the Morrigan, our whole quest is ruined if we do not get it back. We must hunt and kill that monster, but it was impervious to fire, and while we injured it, it took over a thousand arrows and spears and kept walking."

"Show me where it stood, and what direction it came from, and where it went." Master Artrim had long learned, you do not blunder blindly after these creatures. First, understand what they are, then you can resolve a stratagem to trap them.

Chara and Ciera showed him the great footsteps that led in the battle, the blood spilled, and the place it stood when taking the blessed Morrigan. The Witch Hunter leaned down, indicating for his boys to come and inspect things with him.

"You see here, young Cleath - black blood, not yet congealed. Take a sample, do not get any on yourself as it is toxic. Tomic, bring me the copper sheet, let us see if it reacts."

While the team got to work, Chara tugged at Ciera's arm, "He said *Cleath*, Ciera - this has to be the boy who brought down the Twitch. How can we fail when we have such heroes with us!"

All had heard the tale, minstrels had sung it across the country, how a mere stripling of a boy had faced down the greatest of all Twitches, one who had bettered even the great Witch Hunter himself. They sang his praise, they sang his generosity, yet before them was indeed just that - a mere stripling. Ciera was heartened by their presence, but what they had faced was not going to be defeated by anything but a small army. "We are fortunate, Chara," he answered, not wanting his pessimism to show.

Cleath took a drop of the black blood and dropped it onto a copper plate. To his delight, the blood sizzled and baked. "Master Artrim, it is burned by the copper."

"Good, good," the witch hunter sighed. He had seen the energy of the thing, even at a distance, and had hurried forward. Too late to save the Morrigan, but now they had a huge advantage - they knew the creature suffered the same blood weakness as a witch. How it survived out of the mist, he knew not, but he had to suppose it was because the moonlight, in some way, allowed it to exist outside its own domain.

Looking up to Ciera, he explained, "The thing can only move in our world at night. If it does not reach the mist before the sun rises, it will be burned by the morning light. We know this by its blood, so your sacrifices have not been in vain. If we can track it, we can kill it, for we have weapons for which it has no defense. We must move swiftly - Only men with horses can ride with us."

No one would question the word of the greatest Witch Hunter who ever lived. Ciera nodded to his lieutenant to gather as many as they could, "What weapons will we need, Master Artrim?"

"There are still Whytes, and you know how they love the smell of horse. We must take pots of oil, and burning arrows for those. The giant will fall to copper, do you have copper head spears or arrows?" he asked.

Chara frowned, "Yes - yes we do. If we had but known we might have been able to suffice and stop it here."

"Knowing the past is what finds solutions in the present," Pherial Artrim was addressing the lads more than the men. "This is why we study our chemistry. Learning and action combined form the heart of the true warrior."

"This is THE Cleath, the one in the songs?" Ciera could barely contain his joy. From deepest depression, his heart now soared. Surely with such men at his side, they could not fail.

"It is he," replied his Master. "The lad stood where all had failed, including myself. We live because of his courage, but he is not one for words, Master Ciera. We understand Master Jack will be at the Plateau when we are ready to consecrate the Morrigan?"

"Those were his words," answered Ciera.

"Good, we have much to discuss about the nature of the Witches."

"He is the font of all knowledge!" Ciera agreed.

"Blessed be the Master Jack," Pherial responded in kind.

Chara had arrived with twenty-three other men and horse, each with oil pots and weapons strapped to their sides. "We are ready," he stated.

And out they rode, eleven Witch Hunters and thirty-five of the Quest. Ciera left his instructions with the wagon master, a solid reliable fellow, who would follow the guidance he offered. "Test the road where the wheels must go, chock them at every pause, we must not risk the Tor for any reason. Send out scouts to locate any signs of a spring."

As the youth were throwing the dead forms of the Whytes off the edge of the road, the attack party moved out at a canter. The quest must continue, and the risk of any threat was now greatly diminished. The Whytes would not return that night, and by setting off immediately they would make it to the plateau by dawn.

"What signs must we look for, Master Artrim?" Chara pulled up to see if his men could help in the tracking.

"The usual, broken grasses, blood, everything you would do when tracking a wounded animal, but already I see a concern." He points to the trail shifting to the East. "See, the direction it started to take has changed. It was heading directly for the mist, but it has veered off from its straight line. I am thinking you may have wounded it more than you realize."

Ciera commented, "Or the Queen is fighting back, clouding its mind, like what happens in the mist." he suggested.

Artrim agreed, "As well you know, Master Ciera." Then he looks over to Chara, "He would not have mentioned it, but one of the times I caught myself a Twitch, your young Master Ciera was with me. It is why I readily agreed to the request for aid, and I am very glad we did, now we see the fear the witches have of the Morrigan."

He paused and looked behind him at the lads who followed, "What say you Cleath? The Witches fear the Morrigan?"

The boy shook his head, "Nay, Master Artrim. They fear the humans who follow her. They fear what we fear, the loss of territory."

Ciera looked confused, "I do not understand, are you saying that the Witches fear US?"

Pherial looked at his one-time student, now risen so high in the order of things. *Deservedly so*, he thought to himself. "When we defeated that last one, Cleath here formed a sort of bond. She is dead, but she still speaks with him, whispers more like it. It is why he rarely speaks."

Ciera shuddered to consider such a notion, "How can he cope?" he asked, sincerely. "Surely she must be after his mind?"

Master Artrim looked back at the boy, whose eyes were once more looking to the ground. "He suffers many things, the nightmare of that time will never leave any of us. She was the strongest of them all, one of the originals who approached the humans at the end of the blight, when we first came out from the caves. It appears she is a sort of bridge between their world and ours, the boy is seeking to use her and find a path between these impossible places."

Chara whistled low and respectfully, "Such courage," he said.

"Aye, such courage indeed." Artrim agreed. "Let me show you one of the gifts from Master Jack, a thing found in the dark, and which helps us track the beasts." He pulls from his leather side bags a pair of binoculars. "Look through the narrow end, the world will rush up to you, and bring the distance closer."

Ciera looked and was amazed. "It is true, it brings the world close, or do I go to it, in some way? I cannot, for I am on this horse, but perhaps my spirit leaps out, like a vivid dream?" He hands the remarkable tools to Chara, who is likewise impressed and amazed.

"What is THAT?" Chara exclaims, handing the glasses back to Artrim, pointing at something in the distance.

"By the Gods - It is Master Jack! He is leading us in the way to go. Everyone to the gallop, we must follow his sacred hover-bike!" the Witch Hunter shouts.

As they gallop to a thing that is moving in the far distance, Ciera shouts over the beating of the hooves, "What is it we follow?"

"Master Jack found some ancient technology, he showed me the last time we stocked up on the copper nets. It is a machine that flies across the planet faster than any horse, though you sit astride it as if it was one," he called back.

Truly we are blessed, thought Ciera to himself as they pursued the swift arrow-like thing in the distance. One miracle after another, and who could doubt this was the Queen, at work in hidden ways. It explained everything, how the buds knew when to awaken, how the fields knew how to ripen corn. The Queen and her Mother, under the father sky.

A relentless optimism now coursed through his veins. They would achieve this great task, they would be able to keep the evil ones at bay, their world would be made safe. The beating of the hooves drummed over the landscape, the moonlight shone brightly, the soft wind of autumn still carried the scents of summer so recently passed. In less than a month the cold would come, but now he felt sure that by then the youth would be back at their farms - no one would suffer the hunger of shortage.

In six months the river would rise, spreading her bounty over these lands, filling the farms with silt, the rich gift of earth. And he would go back to hunting the ruins for the items of antiquity. But first, they must trap the giant, save the Morrigan, and get her to the plateau - somehow. That would be solvable, it had nothing like the weight of the Tor.

At this point, a thought enters his mind, unbidden, uncalled for. *"Are you certain the witches are your enemy?"* it asked. What magic was this? But that was all, nothing else. Well, they were nearing the borders of the dark lands, and the giant would be controlled by some witch mind - he probably fell into it briefly. But disturbing, even so. He moved his horse closer to Master Artrim, "Can witches call across the plains into your mind this far away?" he asked.

"Oh," he said with a smile, "Cleath has been talking to you, has he?"

"Cleath?"

"Yes, he learned it from the witch. He can speak directly to a person's mind, and he hears the thoughts of others around him all the time now. It is a blessing and a curse, but he KNOWS when a witch is near and can tell us without words. He even knows what level they are, sometimes even their names." Artrim answered.

"They have NAMES? Do the wonders of this night ever cease! Well, he asked if I were certain the witches were the enemy! What a strange question."

Artrim looked up briefly, catching the quest leader's eye as they galloped. "His view is blasphemy according to the views of the tribal leaders, yet they are not the ones in the field catching and killing these creatures. The answer? I do not know. What I know is that a dead one takes nothing from our people and gives much back, so I prefer them dead. We will talk later, for now, the giant and save the Morrigan!"

"Ho Artrim," a voice called out from the right, "I see a large shape moving beside us, maybe a mile away. "

Still at full gallop, he reaches back, gets the binoculars, and stands in the stirrups to look. "Well spotted soldier. There, I see it! The GIANT!"

A roar comes unbidden from the men - Ciera calls out, "Make certain you have a fire set on your saddle, soak your arrows and be prepared to circle the creature and aim at its eyes. This is what affected it the most. Those with copper weapons, follow the Witch Hunters and support them. The rest, harass and take the attention of the monster away from our trapping team."

Each man takes the flint and lights the fuel-soaked cord that will act as a spark to light the oil. They take the arrows, soaking them in the oil pot, and placing them in their quiver - all while they race towards the creature. The battle cry goes up, "Ahhhh yyiiii" they cry.

The creature seems confused, it is limping, dragging one leg behind. Master Artrim calls, "It is too big to net, lads, use copper spears and throw them at that leg. All we have to do is stall it till morning and the sun will do the killing for us."

It turns to face the threat coming towards it, the creature swings its head. It remembers these nasty ants that bite. It wants to fight, but it has to get the rock back. The instructions were to get the little rock from the wagon, bring it back. It makes the decision and starts to hobble faster in the direction it must go. But where is that? It is confused.

Soon the humans fall on it, firing flaming arrows at its one good eye, but it cannot protect itself well, because it must hold this rock. It is heavy, it cannot be held long in one arm - but it must not let it go. Yet it just wants to let it go and run, run away from these bitter creatures. They fall on it from all sides, surrounding it - screams and spears and arrows fly. And then a biting pain, an atrocious pain that causes it to drop the rock.

Faster than you might imagine, it swings about and almost catches one of the nasty creatures, but its hurt leg will not work, and in spinning around it cannot keep balance. It falls - and as it falls, nets fly from everywhere, they burn the skin, they paralyze. The creature squeals in pain.

From the darkness, a voice of authority calls out, "Enough lads, the work is done. It cannot move."

All turn and there stands Master Jack, smiling with pride. "You have done your tribes great honor this day. You have saved the Morrigan, saved the quest, and defeated the monster. The song will be sung for a thousand years."

Master Artrim comes over on his horse and bows. "Surely we should kill it now, while we can, Master Jack?"

"You might, if you don't mind losing a life or three. Once you get in close enough to kill it, it is close enough to kill you, remember. Soon enough the sun will do its work for you, but there is something I want to show you, if you trust me enough?"

"Of course Master Jack, your word is the highest in the land. You are the old one, the wise one, we will heed your voice." Master Artrim looked about as he said the words, all were in agreement.

"Well, we still have to get that heavy little sucker up to the Giza Plateau, and what I see here is the perfect beast of burden to do it."

Ciera is astonished, "Surely you cannot mean to let that thing take up the Morrigan again? It will run back to the witches."

Jack laughed, he loved the common sense of these people. They were so true to their way, and the notion of duplicity or lies, it was almost foreign to their nature. Unlike himself, who was as two-faced and duplicitous as they come - which is why he had been so successful out here in the wilds of Egypt. "So tell me this, why was it wandering about, lost, and heading towards the plateau? The Morrigan already has it, lads, it already owns it. Take off the nets, step back, and watch it take the burden for you."

Master Artrim is somewhat confused, but this is a wise man, he trusts his words. "Very well Master Jack," and he signals for the lads to pull back the copper nets. As they do so, the creature lifts its head, apparently remembering its task once more. "Everyone - get well back from the creature, Master Jack has in some way enchanted it to take the Morrigan to the Plateau."

"Everyone, stand either side and behind the creature, but leave the way towards the Plateau open. We will herd it like we herd sheep - it is a dumb animal, let it be what it is and carry our burden for us." Trader Jack announces in a loud, clear voice.

Of course, they were not to know Cliff had been doing this the whole time, shooting at its feet, pushing it in the direction of the plateau. Nor were they to realize he had hopped onto the bike to do the same for them, to lead them in the direction they needed to go. All this needs remain unspoken, a secret.

Sure enough, the creature struggles back to its one good leg, takes up the Morrigan, and walks in the direction of the Sphinx. Jack loves his little anti-grav scooter, and putters along behind, smiling at the awe these folk feel at such a simple thing as herding an animal. What surprises him is when one of the Witch Hunter children comes over, and looks at him. "You are not as it seems - not at all. You come from over the ocean, from a flying city. You came to help us, this is good."

That was when Jack realized the boy didn't speak. Dammit, a full-blown telepath? This WILL have to go onto the record. He speaks back to the child, "When did you learn this ability, child?"

"The Witch taught me, she still teaches me." he hears in his mind.

Then it clicks, "You must be Cleath, Artrim mentioned you. Well take care child, telepathy goes both ways. As much as you are plugged into another, the other is plugged in to you."

"What are the witches, really?" Cleath asks in his mind once more.

Well, no point trying to hide things from a telepath, "I think they live in a dimension beside ours. Long ago, before the collapse, very dangerous weapons were used in a pointless war. Evil weapons burned the structure of matter itself, releasing side effects that were not properly known. This caused a rift in time and space, and so the Witches as you know them are a civilization that I believe lives in that world we opened ourselves to. Now, it is bleeding into ours."

"They are not evil?"

"They want to survive, we are a threat to them, they are a threat to us. The Morrigan, once in place, will create a field that will start to separate the two dimensions once more."

"Thank you Master Jack. But please, what does this word Duplicitous mean?"

"It is a word to describe a person who lives in two dimensions." he said, smiling broadly.

"Am I therefore duplicitous?" the boy asked, not yet understanding.

Jack laughed, "Not yet child. But as Master Artrim passes to his old age, I am sure you will take over his role, and we will have the chance to speak at length on these subjects. You are the potential solution to many problems, child, and I hope we will be good friends."

The boy rolls his horse around and goes back to the shepherding party. Jack smiles, and busses Cliff on the two-way, "Did you pick up that conversation, Cliff?"

"What, where you were talking to the boy telling him secrets that breach all levels of non-interference. You sure you want that kept in the logs?" he replied.

"Absolutely, what do the psyche reading tell you?"

"Farm me - looking now. Mind blowing - off the goddam charts. What IS that kid?" Cliff is stunned, he has not seen telepathic activity this strong, ever.

"A full-on natural telepath, one you cannot keep secrets from. He already knows where we come from, he knows about our background - he can read your mind like a damn book. Isn't it incredible!" Jack is so happy his face is ready to split with the smile.

"I don't get it?"

"Non-Interference goes two ways, Cliff. Think about it, we keep things hidden to preserve their way of life. We fear we will disturb their natural evolution - but a telepath cannot have secrets, cannot have anything hidden. If we TRY, we will be disturbing HIS natural evolution. So it is my job to cultivate and educate this child. It is now essential we integrate him into the knowledge of our people, our presence, and what we aim to do to help his people. It's perfect!

"This is groundbreaking, it is stuff WE can learn from THEM. The scientists will be falling over themselves to get a research team out here. They will forget about everything else, and just want to understand this little bugger who popped up like a mushroom in a field of shyte. But for now, let's get this frequency generator in place, and have the quest finished. Nice job rounding it up."

"What? No, I did nothing boss. It just made its way in the right direction." Cliff signed off and made his way back to three thousand feet.

Jack Blake had seen and heard many things in his lifetime, but now he was wondering what was happening here. All his plans, over ninety years of them, were slowly coming to fruition. The people were erecting a barrier, believing it on their own merits, yet at the last minute, a complete twist threatens to destabilize it all. And then, the impossible? That creature should have made a clear bee line for the mist, but instead, it works its way to the Giza plateau.

When the impossible happens, you start looking at the implausible for an explanation. And the only implausible solution that worked here was Cleath, the little telepath.

Was the little guy doing what HE did, working unseen in clear view to help his people?

The only true voyage, the only bath in the Fountain of Youth, would be not to visit strange lands but to possess other eyes, to see the universe through the eyes of another ...
Marcel Proust

London Central: Back at the Canter

Mark Bladwell, the CEO at the office of integration at Canter City could not believe the stats. Jack was up to something again, he had to be. The wily old snake had concocted and cajoled whatever he had needed to do what he felt he had to do out there, but a full-blown level five telepath? Occurring in the wild, no training, no guidance? A person would go mad.

They had telepaths, of course. These were used in exploring new worlds - where there was no language these were the only ones who could communicate what the humans were wanting and set up trade arrangements. But they lived in a shielded cabin the whole time, and were only brought out as and when necessary. To imagine a child of that level had survived in a society was one thing, but the thing would be completely mad.

However, you cannot fake psych-reads unless you tamper with the equipment, and while he may not trust Jack, Cliff Trilby was way too smart and too strong a company man to let that happen, and he was in the flitter. There had to be some truth to it.

But if the report was right, if this DID exist, it changed everything. Blake was right, they now had an OBLIGATION to educate the telepath. There had been two natural telepathic races on this planet, the Australian Aborigine and the Malaysian dream people - Both ancient, but that was the whole tribe, all able to understand and know each other's thoughts. A single child, on his own? It changed everything. It was no longer a matter of allowing the tribes to grow in their own way, this one had to be trained.

The child was an asset of inestimable value, and he knew how the psyche-scientists would react - they would ignore any and all rules of non-interference and be out there in droves. Their last telepath just up and died when they got back to Earth, saying it was corrupted, ruined, and that the whispers of the dead were everywhere. Suicide. Despite the shielded room, he went mad. And he was just a level four!

But it was too damn convenient. Jack Blake had finally been irrevocably recalled, and the ONE thing that will keep him out there crops up. Luck of the damn Irish, that one. Bladwell looked out from his platform, a converted life raft from the main ship now kitted out for administration. They had used Jack to salvage so much technology that, allied with the natural make-do attitude of the miners, they were now able to start manufacturing some tech.

The ruin of old London town below was slowly being transformed, first with magnetic domes to control the weather, and now with the shattered buildings being leveled, they could start to look at some sort of productivity from the place. In truth, Bladwell had originally argued for workers to be brought over, as there were too few miners to seriously divide their energies towards self-sufficiency and planetary repair. Jack had solved the problem with organizing produce from Egypt, after the discovery that whatever had blighted these lands had ignored the soils in the Middle East.

But the radionics soaking over everything else had made a real mess. Even today you could still not live on the ground for fear of contamination. Once the oceans heated up, whole life cycles ended. The place was almost devoid of life when they had arrived. The ionic soup that surrounded the planet had done far more than just cut off the sunlight. it had released toxins, created acid rains, no end of trouble. If they had not gotten back when they did, the planet may have turned into another Mars.

Here was the paradox, the land with the greatest disturbance, the alien incursion from the witches, had somehow managed to retain fertile soils and some people. Further, it had gone from desert to an oasis, a place where the acid rains had not fallen. Without this food basket, they would have been on the tasteless crap put out by the synthetic food generators, and no doubt would have abandoned Earth completely to find a more workable planet.

It had been a huge undertaking, clearing the ionosphere, tracking down and repairing what they could of the old tech O2 generators, learning new skills. They were colonizers now, not a returning mining crew. But a TELEPATH - it changed everything.

"You old dog, I don't know how you set this up, but you just made yourself invaluable," Bladwell laughed as he filed his official report. Not too many details, just enough to get what he needed. He had recommended an initial scientific assay be made, first to test the limits of the boy's telepathy and, if found to be genuine, register a proposal to bring him on board with their world. You can't hide anything from a telepath, so there was no point pretending the mining vessel wasn't there anymore.

But a forking level FIVE! Perhaps it was true, that rumor of a boy stopping one of the most powerful witches out there in the mist because only a level five could do that. A knock at the door, "Come in." Bladwell calls out.

The black uniform of the Psyche Squad was unmistakable. "Calling about our little telepath, are we Conrad?"

Conrad Steiger was not an unpleasant man, but neither would you accuse him of pleasantry. He was a square-faced Six Foot ex-rigger who discovered the cushy role of Psyche officer was well paid and gave plenty of time off. He had not one ounce of psychic perception, his job was to protect the ships telepath. In this role, he had a say on security. "Have you finalized your report, Mark?" he asked.

"Just uploaded. You want a copy?"

"Yes, please. So, it is true?"

"The readings need verification, could be error in the equipment. Could be dear old Jack bending reality to suit his purposes, could be many things." Bladwell did not want to appear overly anxious.

"Mark, I could barely handle our last one. He was one weird mother, felt him crawling in my head any time I got inside ten feet of him. Are they going to lump me with another one?" Conrad was concerned for his skin.

Bladwell didn't blame him. Telepaths were difficult at the best of times, but a FIVE, and one not incorporated into their society? It was dangerous. It was also why he didn't include the actual figures in his report. That sort of power meant they could take over your mind, and you would never know it. A level Five could suggest that pointing a pistol at your head and pulling the trigger was a really good idea, and you would do it.

"For the record, Conrad, I am going to recommend that, if this is proven true, that the only course to follow is to keep the boy in his natural environment. Jack can look after him better than we can. We will slowly introduce him into our society, effectively making him a bridge between his tribal world and ours. We will teach him the language, our traditions, culture, that sort of thing. Might resolve some of the difficulties I know the lads are suffering, given a little time."

Conrad knew what THAT hint meant, access to the girls there. "Well, thanks, Mark. I appreciate it. I was worried, I mean, I kinda got the blame for the last guy hanging himself, as if I could have changed anything. But just opening the door to his damn room still causes phantoms to jump around inside me. So, I can go back and say you will be working to resolve the - problem?"

"That is not your only concern. Was there anything specific, Conrad?" You didn't need to be psychic to see he an itch to scratch.

"It is the witch thing. Jembe (the telepath who killed himself) was constantly talking about them, saying they were trying to get into his head. I think they were the reason he killed himself."

"And this boy has had contact with witches, so you are worried he might be controlled by them, and therefore you are asking what sort of damage could he do?"

"Yeah, pretty much. Not just me who is worried, either. There is talk, crazy talk, about going out there and sorting it."

Mark Bladwell knew a warning when he heard it. Steiger was not a smart man, but the man knew he couldn't take this higher up the chain. The miners had to go through their union boss to speak to management. He was letting him know a revolt was in the wind. And it wasn't an unreasonable fear, what a telepath can do is truly frightening. If the child WAS under control by some witch, it was a serious matter. "I hear you, Conrad. The child will not be brought here until it had been vetted and approved. Thank you for the advice. However, on the positive side of the coin, if this works out, it will mean a more open, ah, dialogue with the natives."

That was the news Conrad wanted to take back to the troops. He nodded, then left - message delivered, message received.

Bladwell sat there for long moments, contemplating. Miners were essentially superstitious rednecks, obsessed with omens and charms, and very trigger-happy. Security over flitters was not a high priority, there were precious few humans, and when people had time off they liked to take an anti-grav to the polar regions, anywhere really, just rubber necking.

In Egypt, the flitters were always shielded and the men were not allowed contact with locals, but that didn't stop some heading off to find themselves a girlfriend for a weekend. It got stopped, and tracking bugs now grounded any flitter going into Egypt without permission. It was madness, as overt contact with outsiders would break down the entire society of the people there. Yet it was hard to insist on discipline when every single member of the staff was invaluable, and there were so few humans left. He had been fighting the miners for years, they all wanted to pick up a female child from the outlands, raise them as their own, and in this way get themselves a wife.

No one could blame them, mining ships were mostly men. The sex dolls were OK, but the real thing was much better. However, their notion amounted to stealing a child under the age of two for the express purpose of being cultivated as a sex partner. It was just wrong, no matter how you sliced it. But it was getting harder and harder to regulate men becoming increasingly agitated over what amounted to the confinement of a monastic life.

That was the crux of every difficulty they had, not enough women. The miners saw perfectly good ones out there in Egypt and could see no reason why they had to suffer for some academic concept of not interfering with a nations evolution.

His com flashed, it was Jack Blake, "You read the report?"

Bladwell looked at the weathered face. "You are looking old, Jack. Time to retire."

He laughed, "Yeah yeah, the young bucks would all love to get the chance to gorge on the sweet ones over here, I know. What did you recommend?"

"Devil and the deep blue sea, isn't it? It seems so incredibly fortunate to have this turn up out the blue that I wonder if it isn't rigged. But I have authorized a survey, you will be getting some analysts out there shortly."

"Mark, it is not enough. This kid stared down a goddam TWITCH - it is no joke, Pherial Artrim himself confirmed it. The thing is, what I didn't put in the report, he has an ongoing connection - she is dead, but he is still in contact, she is still talking to him. It is a bridge we are looking at, and maybe some answer to what the fuck happened on this planet when we were away." Jack's eyes had none of his usual humor - Plus, he was still in the field.

"You haven't settled the frequency generator yet?"

"Take a look," Jack swings the viewfinder around as the dawn rose over the horizon. There, one of the creatures from the dark wilds of witch country, a giant no less, was placing the generator down on its spot at Giza. What is more, a little boy is there, touching it, apparently thanking it for its help.

"What am I looking at, Jack?" he asked, not believing his eyes.

"That's the kid - Mark, he can fookin well talk to them, and they OBEY him. He somehow told this creature to bring the generator here to the plateau, after some witch had sent it in to steal it. This has layers of difficulty no second-rate psyche team will resolve. Plus, we now have witches sending creatures out into OUR world, to steal the one thing that will keep them bottled up. HOW did they know this?"

"Do you have a theory?" Bladwell knew the old bugger already had a game plan.

"What I have is a fact - we have TWO evolutions going on here - the Witches are not a side effect of some war, they are their own, unique civilization and they are at war with the people of the plains. We have to broker some sort of peace deal, and the only possibility we have of doing this is with this boy. Do you understand, we need some sort of embassy with the witches, a diplomatic connection."

Bladwell was not surprised, despite the fact he was. He knew Jack would concoct something to make his presence necessary, but an embassy with the witches? "Jack, you are suggesting those blood thirsty monsters that are little more than vampires have a culture beyond rapacious theft of land and destruction of property? I don't see it, and I do not see anyone this side agreeing with you."

"That is the problem, Mark - No one sees the obvious. The kid gave me a clue, a sort of telepathic image, of how the witches see US. Not sure if he intended, but it is what I got - We see them as ethereal vampires sucking off the life energy of the land, yet from THEIR view, we are disconnected apes stumbling about ruining 'their' world. For them, the energy they absorb forms a connection, an intimate attunement with their environment.

"They don't see their actions as desecrating the land, they see they are converting what is to them a wasteland back to a beautiful environment. They hate us, because we destroyed the beauty - That was when we removed the ionic soup. That was their sky - we stole it from them."

"For fucks sake, Jack - That is just insane. If anything, it lends me towards thinking the damn witches DO have the boy." Mark snapped back.

"Is it insane? Consider, we found NO evidence of war, other than some clever new bombs, apparently designed to remove temporal stability. The hatred of the races for each other in the Middle East led to the No Matter bombs - and when they were set off we thought it must have triggered a world war, but the radiation that is everywhere is not nuclear - it is ionic flux. Plus, think about this: We talk of that area as the cradle of civilization, and yet no one has ever come up for a good explanation as to why the pyramids were built."

"Absurd, everyone knows they were tombs." Mark snorted.

Jack Just smiled, "With zero evidence, people believed they were tombs. Why? Because that was the best explanation at the time, just like the damn things were built by Khufu - when the stele clearly says he renovated them. Just as we know the Sphinx is far older than what we were taught, we also know the pyramids date back to ancient astrological alignments, way before Khufu. What's more, they focus on the Pleiades.

"But what do we know from that prehistory? One thing is certain, there was a tremendous flood, the sort that could only occur with a vast shifting of the crust. This event is noted in countless tribes around the planet, so maybe, just maybe, there is more to it. What do you think?"

"I think you been puffing too much of the catnip, Jack." Mark was not having any of it.

"Yeah, well I am not asking you to believe. I am asking you to explain why the entire Earth was decimated, but there is no actual evidence of war outside of Egypt. I am also asking you to explain where the fookin PYRAMIDS have gone, for god's sake." Jack was strident. He had to convince this man about what he was saying before it headed on up the chain.

"Well, that we can guess, they were hit with No Matter bombs. It is the only explanation."

"Exactly, Mark - Precisely that! The Pyramids were zapped from existence, then this ionic soup starts flowing in, destroying everything. Whole countries, all the people, all the animals, swallowed up - EXCEPT for Egypt. THIS place reverses and becomes green and fertile, like it was before the damn pyramids were built. Stop and think without bias - Have you ever considered WHY someone went to all that effort? We know it wasn't a tomb, there are no funeral inscriptions, no items to carry the Pharaoh across to the afterlife, just a sarcophagus, a thing known to be used in their initiation rituals.

"Bladwell, raise your eyes up out of that thick skin of yours and start to see the obvious. My best guess is that someone built the damn pyramids to keep these witches out. I am guessing way back there was some sort of dimensional shift, maybe from the great floods, maybe they CAUSED the floods, who can say - but someone figured out that you needed to build an ionic resonance field right at that spot to stabilize the dimensions."

"Well, that is a huge leap of conjecture mixed with fantasy, Jack. But let's suppose there is something in it, what evidence do you have to support the theory?"

"Mark, you were the one who confirmed the math regarding the placement of the Resonance Generator. We conducted tests and proved beyond doubt that a specific set of frequencies at that specific spot would keep the ionic soup the witches rolled out to conquer the land at bay. Do you know what the pyramids actually were? Resonance Generators - they had a series of different types of rock, electrically conductive and inert layers, sitting over an ozone collection chamber, created by water in caverns underneath the things. Turns out the Pyramids were BATTERIES - huge, powerful, low resonance batteries. And guess what frequency they emitted?"

"You fookin kidding me? The same as we worked out?"

"Think about it, Bladwell - If I had initially told you I got the harmonics from my calculation of the pyramids, you would have laughed. How do you think I came to try those ambient frequencies? Why do you think I tried it on the Giza Plateau? Mark, what really happened was when those mad religious zealots exploded the pyramids they snapped aside the protection from this influence. THIS was when the mist started encroaching - It has been here the whole time but the thing that blocked it was removed. The Giza plateau is some sort of gateway and the resonant frequencies of the Pyramids in some way held it in check."

"The door between Heaven and Hell." Bladwell had a shocking realization that what Jack might be saying could be true - it could be the WHY that explains everything that happened here on Earth while they were away.

"Only our heaven is their hell, and vice versa. Each side is struggling to preserve their way of life, but now it has all changed. Now we have someone who can talk to these creatures, reason with them, find a way where we can live in some sort of harmony." Jack finally felt the message was being received. There was no enemy here other than ignorance.

Bladwell rubs his hand over his mouth, which suddenly felt bone dry. He reached for a beer, pulled it from the fridge, and cracked it. He thought things through for long minutes. Even though Jack was essentially his sparring partner in dealing with the natives, he had enormous respect for what the man had done. Out there, working on his wits, he had stabilized agriculture, brought the natives out from the caves, and given them direction and purpose. "Ok, just for a moment, let's presume you are right - where do we go from here?"

Jack sighs, "Well, for one, we imagine we have gained control of the planet by clearing the ionic soup from the atmosphere - but we haven't. We still have to create mag domes, purify water, and go to extreme lengths to make any ground areas habitable. Only a few places on the planet are not touched, one is Egypt, and I am going to guess that it has a specific resonance in the rock that resists this 'ionic creep' that has blighted the rest of the world. Only THREE places are left that are free of it, Mark - the center of what used to be Australia, and a small section around what was once Minneapolis.

"And what is the common thread in all these areas? Pangaea Rock, the original surface of the planet. It cannot be a coincidence. Mark, it looks to me like our witches have been here a long, long time. Millennia ago, we developed a technique to stop their dimension bleeding into ours, a thing we are about to replicate in the next hour. What I want from you, if this works as we expect, is a hand picked crew of MY choice to come here and study it. That's all I need, people I can trust, but more importantly, people with the right energy to work with our little Cleath here." Jack already had a soft spot for the kid.

"Yeah, the kid. How do you know you can work with him and stay in charge? There's no record of anyone dealing with the level Five before, they don't live past childhood." Bladwell had done his research, only a few recorded occurrences, and every one of them ended in disaster.

He sighed, "He is a special one, Mark, not one drop of deceit or violence in his blood. I spoke with Pherial at length on the way to the plateau and he confirmed, the way Cleath trapped the Twitch, their most powerful creature, was by loving the damn thing so much it couldn't move. That was when the penny dropped, I realized WHY it became fascinated - they had seen US as the barbarians, the invaders, the interlopers - but here was one who loved them. It fascinated her, how was such a thing possible?"

Mark shook his head, "Yeah, but have you considered that maybe this is part of their dance. To build our confidence. Maybe they already own the kid? They are as cunning as a shytehouse rat."

"Mark, to get what this is, you would have to know what it is like to feel total acceptance. That is the reality of what this boy has, I can't explain it, but whatever it is, he has it. There is ONE constant in the language of the universe - You cannot despise or distrust anyone or anything that deeply accepts you. His strange compassion has formed a bridge, one we can work with.

"What is more, I believe him when he says she still speaks with him and wants a dialogue. I think both parties, both humans and witches, have been deeply complicit in an ongoing fabrication of what we believe the other side to be," Jack cracked a beer himself from his kitty, and tipped it up as a salute to Mark.

Mark raised his in equal measure. IF he was right about this, Jack Blake just solved an impossible puzzle. He knew where he was going with it, open up a dialogue via the telepath, then negotiate a treaty, just as they had always done on every planet they mined. Resolve to declare defined areas and zones pertinent to either party. "It is a huge ask to bring everyone else along with this, Jack, but I will do my best. We need to give this theory a red hot crack, because, as you say, the telepath changes everything."

"Doing our best isn't enough, Mark. We just DO it. And we do NOT need everyone coming along, your authority is sufficient. Organize me a posse of like-minded, free thinking scientists, and give me the right to pick and choose the final members of the team. This is within YOUR orbit. You approve the program I just put forward and no matter who agrees or disagrees with the notion, they can't change it. Once we can start negotiations, once they see infected areas rolling back, the rest will believe - before that, they will snort just like you did and say hogwash. Can you give me this, Mark?"

Mark Bladwell looked at the screen for a long moment. He ran over every parameter, every argument he would have to counter, every person he would have to cajole. "If the stats show Cleath is a genuine level Five. If the radionic harmonics you set up work. And finally, if the witches are kept in check and no further incursions result, you will get what you want, Jack."

"So, you are finally starting to see what I have been doing out here all this time?"

Mark Bladwell had to admit, the bastard had been right. "Yeah, kudos to Trader Jack and his world of deception. "

Jack laughs a deep, hearty laugh, "Necessary deception, Mark. But one that will soon not be needed. It will make everyone happy if we can sort this - win-win all the way round. I will get back to you after the setup with the results."

"OK, if we are going to tell a few stories, let's only attract as much attention to this project as we need. Truth is, I have already fudged the figures and presented your little guy as a level Four. If we rate him higher we won't be able to keep the parasites away from trying to suck up every ounce." Bladwell had instinctively known he would have to go along with Jack on this one. The fact was, a level Five? No one thought it possible. If the boy really was this, his duty to the human race was to develop and encourage the child, which meant keeping it out of the hands of the scientists.

As he went to sign off, sunlight broke the horizon in Egypt. He watched as it streamed onto the beast that had stolen the Morrigan. With the boy there, touching it, speaking to it, the thing evaporates into the mist that it was formed from, a mist that floats helplessly away on the breeze.

Mark Bladwell didn't want to believe it, but he was becoming a believer.

ooo0000ooo

There on the plateau of Giza, the place where we might argue human civilization commenced, Jack Blake looked at the extraordinary crew that had come together to make this a reality. The old witch hunter, Pherial Artrim, one of his earliest friends - He came to the outpost, distraught about his father and the witches. The rolling coin thing was the inspiration of Paddy O'Shea, those coins were small resonance chambers, and the action of rolling them set up harmonics that drew the attention of a witch.

This day belonged to Patrick, he was the one who trained Pherial, he was the one who guessed that the witches could be controlled with ionic resonance. Without his brilliance, who knows where they would have ended up.

He handed out beers to all, praising the sun as it rose, praising all who had gone before to make this happen - most especially, with a tear in his eye, he lifted a beer, "To Paddy O'Shea - the first of the Witch Hunters and my friend. You, my dear friend, opened the door to this moment - I hope you are watching."

Pherial Artrim lifted his beer, "To Patrick O'Shea, the man who taught me everything I know. He is the reason we are here today!"

After the cheers, Ciera lifted his beer, "To Master Jack, our friend and companion. The one who has shown the light of our path and given us our truth!"

Jack comes back with a hand, waving down the celebrations. "We will spend the next few days thanking everyone for everything. Let us fire up this sucker and see if it works, then we can pat each other on the back!"

"How do we do this, Master Jack?" Ciera was deeply puzzled. Everything they had done was based on their collective faith in this man. He had never let them down, never failed them. He was their guiding star, but he kept his secrets to himself, and rarely let them out into the open like he was about to right now.

"Ah well, you remember when I first told you of the Morin and the Morrigan, you had brought me an ancient recording device?"

"I remember it like yesterday, Master Jack," Ciera replied.

"Well, the Morrigan needed to be in the correct place, a spot where the frequencies of the world blend in the right mix with the inner and outer dimensions - that is here, at Giza. It is an ancient place, where giants from the past would meet and plan the fate of mankind. It was they who built the Sphinx, whose gaze we passed under coming here. Now, please sing along and help the awakening of the Morrigan."

With this, he pulled the ancient I-pod out of his rucksack and connected it to a pair of small but powerful speakers. Then he pressed a button, and the anthem of man started playing: Leonard Cohen and his song, Hallelujah.

Now I've heard there was a secret chord
That David played, and it pleased the Lord
But you don't really care for music, do you?
It goes like this, the fourth, the fifth
The minor falls, the major lifts
The baffled king composing Hallelujah

Hallelujah, Hallelujah
Hallelujah, Hallelujah

Your faith was strong but you needed proof
You saw her bathing on the roof
Her beauty and the moonlight overthrew her
She tied you to a kitchen chair
She broke your throne, and she cut your hair
And from your lips she drew the Hallelujah

Hallelujah, Hallelujah
Hallelujah, Hallelujah

Well, maybe there's a God above
As for me all I've ever learned from love
Is how to shoot somebody who outdrew you
But it's not a crime that you're here tonight
It's not some pilgrim who claims to have seen the Light
No, it's a cold and it's a very broken Hallelujah

Hallelujah, Hallelujah
Hallelujah, Hallelujah

It was a song Jack had taught them all from his earliest of days, a song of praise, a some of joy, a song of deep belief. There was not one child in this new world who did not know the blessed Cohen, one of the Saints of the Old Age. And as they lift their voices to sing in harmony, as they pour their love into the music, the Morrigan lights up! More than this, she starts to float! The heavy, rectangular stone defies reality as the wisdom and life of the Queen enters into the Morrigan to awaken her vessel. Then the Morrigan starts to hum in a frequency that is in perfect resonance with the song.

Ciera is blessed beyond words. Tears flow, all the trials, all the tribulations, everything he had survived and conquered was now vindicated. The strange looks of his fellows as he went into the ancient ruins, the jeers of his peers, that laughter of his people as he pursued the connection to the mysterious Master Jack. All of his life was now proven to be true and just.

The invisible energy of the Morrigan began to pulse and flow as waves of subtle radiance danced across the landscape. Then, when it reached the mist, the vapor backed up, forming a wall against the pulsing harmonics emanating from the Queen. The men all cried out in awe and delight, to see the power of the Queen! Her song would save them all!

Even Jack smiled. Dammit, but it actually worked!

oooOOOOooo

It was late that afternoon when the great Tor rolled up. Morin and Morrigan, united once more! Since the comprehensive conquest of the Whytes, there had been little by way of threat. Just a few weak spots in the road that they avoided. A spring WAS found, which was excellent as it will be necessary for pilgrims coming to this sacred place. Jack had contacted Cliff, who had been beaming information back to the canter all day, showing how effective the frequency modulator had proven to be. It absolutely changed the landscape. Sadly, Jack realized the side effect of saving the world would probably be the same as what happened last time, the Sahara would return and only the strip of land fed by the Nile would remain fertile. But that was hundreds of years away.

Small price to pay for a healthy world.

As to placing the great Tor, rather than risk accidents at this late stage, Jack said he would call on the power of the Morrigan to place the Tor into position. He had already positioned anti-grav plates underneath it, but he DID use the frequency generator to activate them. There was an intense look of awe on the faces of the tribesmen as the monstrously heavy artifact lifted from the trailer and floated into position, where the great pyramid had once stood.

Now, the real reason for the enormous Tor being brought here was made evident, as Jack dialed up adjustments and raised the Morrigan to the very top of the 'upraised hand'. Thus placing it out of the way from any passing creature or even the odd giant who might try and survive the harmonic resonance. Cliff would secure it later, when everyone had gone.

"I reckoned you would be happy with the choice of song to activate this beasty, Leonard," Jack said to the long dead poet. More to the point, it was an anthem everyone knew and could sing when they came to this place. There was a method to the madness, the resonant field needed recharging regularly, and rather than have a team to constantly monitor it, people singing the code song would do this. Resonance is activated by perfect harmony and, as you sing the song that triggers it, you hear notes being 'created' all around you. It is truly a magical experience, one that will affirm the legend of the Morrigan. This place will hold true for many, many generations.

Jack smiled, there was still so much more to do, but this installation at Giza was the one great thing that would protect the people. He almost regretted that inside a few generations, education would come and the young would learn of the science that made this happen. Mystery is not a bad thing, handled properly it can show people to a new day. But ongoing ignorance was never a tonic, and so ignorance must slowly be educated out of the people.

The Witch Hunter called up to his tent as the day closed, "A momentous day, Master Jack. A day we might all be proud to say we were a part of."

Jack waved him in, offering the old man some Arak, which he gratefully received. "The boy ..."

Pherial nodded, "The boy," he agreed.

Jack smiled, "You can come in, Cleath."

Level Five telepaths were not like other people. If they wanted you not to see them, you didn't, but Jack had felt him at his heels the entire day, watching him, observing his communications. Not with a sense of prying, just an endless curiosity. Cleath appeared to materialize in front of them.

"You knew I was here?" he asked of Master Jack.

"I come from a place where your gift is not unknown, we just do not advertise it," the old trader laughed. "For my ancestors, a talent such as yours was a thing all shared. How else do you think I have been able to do deals, help people, shape this world to what it is today?"

"And this is what I must do?" Cleath asked.

"If you choose it. By our meeting here today, beside me with the most respected elder in your world, I would nominate you to follow me, Cleath. To take my role, and to be a bridge for your people." Jack had known it the moment he saw the boy, his protégé'.

"But we must do far more, we must talk with the Ethereals, come to agreements. Working with your people will be a small task compared to this." The boy had a sense of urgency.

Perhaps he sensed the reticence from the Canter? "I am arranging for a team to help you, young Cleath. Plus we will develop machinery that will enable safe transit into the mist, where you can speak and negotiate with the witches without risk, presuming they wish to speak, of course." Jack looks over to Pherial, "There has been a striking development, one where we are coming to understand the witches are not as they seem. We may soon not need the service of the Witch Hunters, old friend."

Pherial was not surprised. "Even since Cleath defeated the one who destroyed my father I feel the hatred that burned in me fading. It would be a good thing not to lose more children to those creatures, and if we can create a safe world without the need to hunt them, this I will offer no objection to."

Things were changing. Placing the Frequency Generator would irrevocably alter the balance of power between the natives and the miners. It will never be what it was. Time to start revealing the truth of his role here. "As you both know, I am not from the tribes. Have you not thought to ask of where I came from?"

"We see the machine that arrives out of the invisible spaces, that collects the goods you trade. We always presumed you came from where it lived." Pherial spoke as a matter of fact. "It would be foolish to think you worked here all these years to no purpose or profit."

Jack laughed, all that secrecy and they had already guessed at the truth of it. He loved these people. "Good. Well, more will come, to help Cleath negotiate a treaty with the Witches. If successful, we will have made the planet safer which will allow the expansion of the tribes." He looked directly at Cleath, "But you, young man, a great deal will rest on your shoulders. Many tests will come, many obstacles must be crossed, and your patience will be stretched."

He had to consider carefully the next words, but it needed to be out in the open."Have you experienced the NEGATIVE side to this power of hearing people's thoughts, Cleath?"

"To have them do what I will them to? Is this what you mean? That is against the law, and the truth is, I have no heart to force someone to do my bidding. There is little joy in it." he responded.

"Indeed, there is no joy in it at all." Jack smiled thinly. Though he knew the boy might think differently when coming against the stubborn selfishness of the miners. He also knew - just a moment of weakness and a level five could fire out and wipe one of their minds clean. He also knew the fear they would feel meeting this child, knowing what he could do. If Cleath slipped and accidentally let a Psy-blast out, then the fear and hatred against him would build to impossible levels.

Of course, he may as well have spoken it aloud, for the boy nodded severely. "I hear your warning, Master Jack. Thank you for your wisdom."

The old man sighed, "Alright then, next week your people get to see my people. I have to go back tomorrow to organize everything, but it might be best if you all camp here. Many of your people will start to flock to this place, and a strong presence to organize things will be necessary - kitchens will need to be built, housing erected. The only thing, we must keep any development outside the immediate area of the plateau, we need to ensure there is nothing to interfere with the Morrigan. I will show you tomorrow where to establish the village"

Cleath spoke, "Master Jack, may I come with you, to make sure we have the right team?"

Jack looked at the child, he had wanted to spare all the candidates exposure to their little miracle, but he was right. Just open the doors, no more secrets. They will swim or they will drown. "If the Master Artrim releases you, of course."

As the eventide sang with cicadas, all three sat with their thoughts. In the background, the Morrigan hummed on its pedestal, radiating calm, stillness, and security. "Perhaps at last peace will come to this land," Master Artrim suggested. "Of course, the boy may go wherever he pleases. An apprentice is not bound to the word of his master, more especially so when he is apprenticed to a trade no longer needed! We can but hope so."

"What will you do, Pherial?" Jack asked. All the old warrior knew was battle, going into the mist every week, it was a second home for him.

"If young Cleath here is correct, I will be begging for forgiveness. Otherwise, I will live as long as I might. War forces a man to choose between family and purpose, you cannot have both. Without war, I would choose a family, to watch the young grow, to harvest the fields, to happily be a nobody of no importance." The old man laughed, "I wonder, is it too late for domestic bliss? What say you, Brother Jack?"

"We have both battled in the long war, not just against the Witches, but for the soul of the people we love. You will never be forgotten, Brother Artrim, for you forged hope when there was none, you inspired courage where there was fear, but most of all, you found Cleath - a diamond in the dust. Together we can now hope to save this planet. But do I see you on a farm with grandkids running around your feet while you slumber in a rocking chair? No, I see you being part of the community that ventures into the mist to bring the compromise we need. As to family, there is no shortage of pretty things who would happily be the mother to your children."

"And the rest of the lads?" Pherial asked. "They have no trade but the witches."

Jack considered the future, "We will still require the Gregorians for protection, Pherial. As far as I can see, this will not be an easy path, one highlighted by the distinct difference between our negotiating power, which will cause concern. We know nothing about them, they seem to know everything about us. Further, the witches cannot come to us, so we must go to them. This is our fundamental point of leverage in all negotiations, it is also a core area of distrust. While I have faith in the good intentions of Cleath and a strange, displaced sense of acceptance of the one he dominated, we cannot be so certain about the rest - I am thinking we will need every trained witch hunter to assist us, to protect the company as it makes journeys into the mist.

"It would be wrong to imagine all witches and Twitches are the same or have the same goals like the one in contact with our boy. Yes, she was one of the leaders, but we all know how it is, one falls, another rises. It will take years to convince this race of shadows that their best interest is a compromise, a sharing of the planet. It is not a war, but it is not yet a peace."

The two-way comes to life, it is Cliff. "Boss, good news. Mark Bladwell has stamped his authority on the council and commandeered the right to put in a negotiating party. You remain in charge of the operation on the ground, he remains in charge of supervision back at the ship. His first request is to see if we can arrange a clear with Britain, first and foremost, as that will cement the deal."

Jack smiled. This was the first hundred years out of the way. Now for the next century. He turned to Pherial, "What I am thinking is that we give everyone involved in negotiations a bit of a tour of what we are fighting for. So before we go into the field I will show you holographics of our ship, and explain how we came to be here. You will LOVE it."

Dialogue

Negotiations were arduous, steeped in distrust and a degree of mutual loathing. Whoever this race was, where they came from, the purpose or means by which they arrived on Earth, none of this was made clear. They did not share the human desire to know their opponent, nor did they eschew the concept of sharing.

They only obeyed one law: *Strength*. The strong will rule. Their point of respect came from the Morrigan, a technology that was able to keep them spreading their ionic web over the land. It was strong, yet the entire notion of meeting and discussing was proof that those who came from the human side were weak. After several weeks it became clear to Jack that any sort of traditional treaty was not going to happen.

When Jack asked, via Cleath, if they wished the battle with the witch hunters to continue, they were eager for it to be so. They LIKED the challenge and did not fear dissemination or the loss of lands. Gradually an understanding grew, these Ethereals did not think of the human existence as real. *Did they believe their OWN existence was real?* Their answer: Where they went to after this was all that mattered - HOW you lived here determined how you lived there.

"Like the Vikings," Jack had explained to the negotiating party. "These witches have their own Valhalla, and dying in battle ensures a high place at the table in the afterlife. They have no interest in trade, no concept of curiosity about another species, and we are only talking because they know the Morrigan can be turned up and push them back further."

Cleath had grown, not physically, he was a tiny thing, but he had gathered in stature and power. As he came to understand the ability and fine tune his gift, he also took the advice from Master Jack to keep it secret, to not reveal anything of his true power - The boy was there with the negotiating team in the mist only in the role of a negotiator. But things were at an impasse. Jack was beginning to grasp why the ancient Egyptians built structures of such power they pushed these things completely out of this dimension.

"Cleath," he asked the boy, " Let me ask this a different way, how do we focus them on agreed boundaries that are mutually beneficial, but which they will see as a win? Further, how do we gauge what they NEED as opposed to what they WANT? We know nothing about them and have no idea what they value. We don't even know how long have they been here, on Earth."

"They do not have the same sense of time as we do, Master Jack. But when I ask their Queen I see a great duration, not time as we know it, but a great duration. The same goes for wealth, the more you control the better off you are, but they don't NEED it, they just WANT it."

Jack stops and thinks for a long time. And what he is mostly thinking is how none of this would be possible without Cleath. He signaled a thought, asking how he was doing. He receives back a clear impression of happiness. The child is pleased to be of service to his people. There has to be an answer in what they see as their purpose.

"So TIME is not an imperative. Wealth as we know and understand it does not exist for them. I get it, so what is it their NEED?" And as Jack asked this, a light dawns, "Cleath, your Queen died in battle, yet she is not in their Valhalla, why is this?"

He is silent for long moments, clearly deep in contemplation. "She does not know." Then he added, "Something about wanting to stay with me."

"Yeah, she fell in love with the greater force. Common occurrence, Stockholm syndrome." Then he gathered his thoughts, and voiced a notion to the tribe, as he called the negotiation group. "Is the concept of negotiating with their belief in an afterlife something we can work? Cleath, what I am thinking is that your Twitch is still conscious, still communicating - and clearly not in Valhalla as she should be. We must be able to build on this - suggestions?"

The little dark-eyed girl, Moni, spoke, "They are aware that Cleath communicates with her, so they must already realize she is not in their Valhalla. Yet, I suspect they are so totally self-centered that the notion that same would happen to them just does not occur. It SHOULD challenge their beliefs, but it does not."

Though young, she was an expert in applied philosophy. A peculiar branch that suited the job, as it took a practical view on conceptual notions. As an example, they came here expecting that the other side would be interested in brokering a deal. They were not. They were merely testing for weakness, like a snake tastes the air for the scent of fear.

Charman, another young graduate, already a Professor of History, suggests, "Perhaps they need to see a demonstration of strength. I understand this goes against the principles of negotiation, but as this is the language they understand, perhaps it is appropriate?"

"What do they see as strength?" Jack asked. "After all, they see killing each other as sport, but they DO have a hierarchy." The light dawns, how stupid of him. " Of course, the obvious - if they come to an AGREEMENT with us, they have been dominated. Suggestions?"

Pherial laughed, "I was wondering when you would see this, Brother Jack. After decades of killing them, I know them well. It is a culture of domination. The strongest mind wins - Perhaps we need a sort of games, a competition, the winner determines a specific result, based on a wager before it starts."

Jack was intrigued, the idea sounded like it might work. "What sort of games do they play? Cleath, do you have a read on this?"

The boy looked at him, "They dominate the other by taking control of their mind. That is their only game, so to speak. The strongest mind wins."

Jack looks at the boy for long moments, searching for an answer to their impasse. "The obvious is staring us in the face. They don't all kill each other, do they? There is a point of balance in their mind battle where one wins and the other loses, so there is a concept of surrender - so there must also be demarcation zones - Surrender to get what? This witch has that area, that witch has this area. They MUST have a sense of property tied to determining an outcome to a battle."

Jack remembered some of his ancient history, a curious tale that came out at the time of the discovery of Tutankhamen. "I read in a novel that the priests in Ancient Egypt used to have psychic battles, I thought it was just a writer's notion. But perhaps the author was tuning in to something that happened. Perhaps the Ancient ones in this land did exactly this, went into mind battles with the ethereal energies - If this is so, we have two of the greatest mind warriors right here!" He looked at Cleath and Pherial.

Charman notes, "It was well known that the Egyptian army targeted the mind of the enemy, not just the body. In point of fact, they stated that a body can wear armor for protection, but the mind cannot. A great deal of their warfare was psychological."

Moni blinked, becoming very animated. "They will go for such a concept, everything about them is competitive. The question is, how do you determine a prize?"

Ferial Artrim laughed, "That is simple, land. It is the only thing they value."

"What do we offer in exchange? What are THEY competing for?" Charman asked.

"Plus, do they have a concept of geography, Pherial?" Jack asked. "Specifically, can we agree to fight for Britain, as one example?"

Cleath was the one who responded, "They can switch off their presence in any one area, or should I say, withdraw to the inner world where they had always existed. The witch within me, she lives on because I feed her attention, thoughts, and dare I say well-wishing. They ALL live on energy, so I am asking if there is an energy they would respect that we can offer in exchange?"

Jack looked at the child, "What specifically can we offer them that they would desire?"

Cleath had a faraway look, gazing off into some distant universe. After some time, he came back, with an understanding. "When we fought and won an area in the past, we cleared the land for farming. As a result, our people created and sang the song of the battle. Each day in that area, the people gifted the lands would sing that song - Of those who fought, those who died. I had not realized but in this way, our people feed their presence. This is an acceptable exchange to them."

Master Artrim considered the words deeply, "Interesting young Cleath, we have presumed they fight for land. Perhaps they fight for glory?"

He confirmed, "In the battles to come, where Master Artrim and the Gregorians face the witches, meet them mind to mind, and defeat them, we will take territory. In return, those who then farm that territory will sing the song of the battle and give praise to the combatants."

Jack just looked at Pherial, who gave a grave nod of agreement. He seemed to believe there was something to this. "They would surrender all of Britain for a SONG?" He is thinking of Indians handing over Manhattan for beads. At the same time, he also recalled that the Indians who handed over the territory didn't own it - but they took the beads. People laughed at how stupid they were, but in truth, the white people were the ones being fooled. So, how was it THEY were being fooled?

Pherial laughed as he explained the simplicity of what Cleath suggested. "The Ethereals will still exist there, but in the subtle realms. The mist allows them to emerge into our existence, where they come to harvest energy, just as we harvest crops. Singing songs will feed them the psychic force they need so they no longer have to hunt for it. They will not NEED the territory if they are being fed by song."

Jack started to get the notion. When they withdraw their presence, the ionic charge would diminish, the land will become arable, and people will be able to populate it. The miners taking away the ionic cloud have made the place unpleasant to live in anyway, so they lose nothing, yet still gain what they need. The Humans lose nothing with a song while the Ethereals gain everything THEY need. This was an agreeable and legal basis for a contract.

"So be it," he said. "How do we set this up?"

Cleath was quiet for a moment, speaking with his inner witch, then looked up, "THIS is what they were waiting for."

oooOOOOooo

The battleground was set at the end of the mist. The witches issued no rules, no framework, no time frame other than, 'When Venus is conjunct the Sun" - Jack and his team did the research, and got the basic framework. They now had a time and place. In Ancient Egypt, at specific astrological times such as this, a psychic battle was held in the old courts, between the various priestcrafts. The sect of the winning priests would hold the ear of Pharaoh for the coming year. However, perhaps the real reason was to do with the Witches?

He asked his history professor, "Charman, do you imagine that the Witches may have in some way channeled through the ancient priests of Egypt? That they were resident in the temples?"

The young man considered the notion for a time, looked up a few reference libraries on his plex, and finally answered, "The ancients certainly believed their brand of God was housed in the various temples built for them. There is nothing specific to connect this to our Ethereals, Master Jack (the team had fallen into the same habit as the locals) yet the feel of this is there. Certainly, a culture does not expend vast sums of money in building religious structures for no reason - The purpose given was that the temples held Egypt in a balance and prevented negative powers from taking over. It was seen this power came through the minds of the people, so given what we have, entirely possible."

Jack thought of the old world, every suburb in every city had a place of prayer, of worship. It was believed by the old religions that the presence of these kept Satan at bay, locked in his realm. It was the reason every church had a bell, with the belief that ringing it cleared the land of Demons.

It was a clue. For now, they would move forward on the suggestion of a battle.

Iron Mist

It was an iron-grey mist they entered. He had gone in long ago with Paddy but had forgotten the sense of desolation it imparted. Jack shuddered, "Like a Bukowski poem" he muttered as they ventured into the sparring grounds. The emptiness was a palpable pressure that seeped into your mind, a sort of hopelessness washing you with venom. He wondered how people like Pherial Artrim survived with his sanity after so many years of this. "How long has it been since you first went in with Patrick, Pherial?"

The old man looked up, war beaten though he may have been outside, here in the mist he took on a new life and barely looked his ninety years. "Some eighty cycles around the sun, Master Jack. I was but a boy when Master O'Shea showed me this path."

"And it doesn't depress you, being in this murk?" Jack questioned.

"My purpose drives me, Master Jack. Here IS my purpose. This day is my destiny, how could I be anything but joyous?"

"Cleath, how do you feel coming into this soup?" Jack asked the boy.

"It may surprise, Master Jack, but I feel a relief here. Outside the mist, all I feel is the constant pressure of thought - minds and feelings constantly calling out. In here, it is different - yes, there is a whisper of threat, but there is also a calm stability. It has its own beauty."

Like a morgue is calm and stable, thought Jack, sardonically. He saw nothing here that could be described as uplifting. He had wondered why Patrick loved it so much, so he supposed there must be some benefit to it.

Cleath laughed, "The plate glass fragility of this world is fascinating. The creatures, all obedient to the strongest mind, and the witches that control them - I wondered why they existed, now I know. This desperate mist we see? From THEIR view, it is like a sunny brook, filled with fruit trees and flowers. For the Ethereal, the frequency, the harmonic, is everything. It is their food, their blessing, their nurture. They see OUR world as a lack, worse, as a riot of madness needing the calm of their mist."

There were just the three of them - Pherial advised against any others, especially the research team as it would tempt the witches to subjugate their minds. Jack need not remind them that the stakes were high, Britain itself was the wager - against their lives. Of course, London agreed quite readily - It didn't seem a bad deal to them, they could only win and no one minded the cost of losing Jack and some natives. He had stayed well out of this world after Paddy died, but once you ventured back into the mist you could TASTE the apathy or the conquered creatures, just as you could feel the sharp brightness of the controllers, a knife poised to strike.

"Your life is your life. Know it while you have it. You are marvelous. The gods wait to delight in you," Pherial quoted a Bukowski poem. "This IS the mist for me, Brother Jack, tinged with a fear and respect for what it holds."

Jack's ears perked, he had forgotten he had lent the old witch hunter books to read. But it was apt, this place was a landscape belonging to the olong dead poet.

The research was unclear, it appeared there were several Egyptian rituals to do with a psychic battle, and all Jack could ascertain was that an agreed time and place, a battle would ensue. How it started, how it ended, even how you determined a winner was unclear.

A bright thought cut through the grey like a beam of sunlight, "We will be good, Master Jack."

The irrepressible Cleath, a bonfire of good cheer and hope, despite the desolation all around them. One might have thought a youth would have suffered a loss of innocence or found a jaded cynicism coming into these barren wastes, but quite the opposite. Jack asked, mind to mind. *"So, might I ask why you are so certain this will work out well?"*

He felt the self-assured smile impressing itself into his soul. His pessimism started to lift as the certainty of the boy's spirit filled him. He felt Pherial beside whispering in his mind. *"It is a truly remarkable thing we have discovered with young Cleath. Who could have imagined conversations without words? In here I can hear everything, I suppose like he does."*

Jack nodded inwardly, *"Level Five Telepath, 100% connection 100% of the time, even in sleep. It is a miracle he survived, and even more of a wonder how he thrives in this misery."*

"This place is a blessing," Cleath added to his thoughts. *"Once my fear left, I understood the purity of this world, its silent perfection. Other than the need for the natives to dominate, it is particularly peaceful here."*

Jack received the image, not one of bleak greyness, but a uniform simplicity - a calm, even place where all things were harmonious. But of course, there were the predators, the mind hunters who looked to take your thoughts and control your volition. "You have no fear of these?" he asked.

"Respect is not fear." Cleath answered.

Pherial laughed openly, attracting a buzz of energy. Jack was starting to understand this place, energy was not suppressed so much as absorbed. The blanket of ions energized the land to the frequency chosen by the controlling Witch, to make them more able to connect with and take the energy of the living things within it. He got the image of a nervous system, the central brain being the controlling witch, and the fibers of her control were the nerves radiating out, connecting to every single thing in her domain.

"We walk in the body of a witch?" Jack was genuinely surprised. He had always considered these wastelands as a corruption of life, not a supporter of it. He was getting it, slowly, this understanding the boy had gleaned.

Pherial's thoughts echoed his, "We walk in the body of the witch," he affirmed. "She feels everything in her domain, like a spider on a web, and we are juicy bugs walking into her parlor. At last, we come to the chosen battle ground."

The Resonance generator had pushed the mist back over seventy miles and they had been dropped off by Cliff at the border, near the area picked by the witches in the old town of Suez, on the canal. Before them stood the remains of an old coliseum-like structure, what would have been a sporting stadium in its day. Master Jack looks ahead, there is no turning back once they step into that place, and no idea what surprises the witches have in store. "Nothing for it but to move on it, I suppose," he whispered under his breath - but his softly spoken words appeared to almost be a shout, one that echoed impossibly in the environment.

Pherial said nothing. Grim faced, he checked his backpack for nets, coins, and witch hunting paraphernalia. Satisfied, he strode directly through the gates, and into the heart of the sporting arena. Was that rustling sound as they entered applause? Jack could feel the sense of awe, of occasion, and it seemed to be coming from thousands of vacant, staring ghosts that sat in the bleachers surrounding them.

He supposed after some eighty years, Pherial was somewhat of a star performer, an athlete of sorts in their world. No attention was paid to the young boy trailing him just as little was paid to himself, other than he felt a keen intelligence observing them all. A test? Yes, a test.

Without warning or fanfare, a shifting occurred in the ether, Pherial immediately came to a stop, and Jack saw he had plucked a GOLD coin from his waistcoat. As he did so, a form shifted from between the atoms, and took shape, a whisping hand reaching out to take the witch master by the throat. And it would have, except the WILL of the hunter forced it to stop. Jack had never experienced such a thing, though surely Patrick had spoken of it, spoken of it as an ultimate thrill.

Was this something like sex for these creatures? It had a sensuous wishing, a transparent desire for union, though a deadly one. Pherial had his eyes closed, intent, focused while the thing moved around in a trance, singing a strange melody of conjoined notes. It was fascinating, watching the Ethereal seeking to draw the witch hunter into her dream, willing his submission to her lust. Pherial was unmoved and began cycling the coin through his fingers, like a magician, waiting for her to come close.

And as she moves in, like a kiss, he sweeps it up, touching her skin with its metal, and she shrieks, seeking to run. But he had her, holding her mind with his mind, and slowly he plunges the coin into the mist. A shrieking, a moan, and whisper, and hatred, all breezes from the grey world around them. And the thing is gone.

But there is no parting of the mist, was this was just a test? To ensure they were worthy for the next performer? Jack was starting to understand, this was a performance, like the Romans and their gladiators. "Part one of the dance," Jack whispered, as Pherial loosens a net from his pack, getting ready for the next one.

"They rarely try direct sex," he said, his words were like thunder as he spoke aloud in this space. And then he laughed, he laughed like the thunder itself, or so it seemed. "NEXT!" he called out. He stood there, utterly confident - Possessed of power and truth, a gospel man standing before the devil, casting him out.

And the next was nothing like the first - a blatant strike from behind them, a pure blast of mind force, driving the witch hunter forward with the unexpected attack. But he turned like a cat, facing the creature. It was difficult to make it out, but the energy was that of some arching dragon, breathing pain and suffering from its nostrils. Here the truth of the witch hunters emerged, for from Pherial an equal monster emerged from what seemed a nothingness, forming a shield to protect the party.

Another strikes from a different direction, but the hunter appeared to expect it, and his phoenix, as his apparition now appeared to be, curled around covering them all from the psychic blows. He looked to Cleath, who nodded, then cast a copper net in the direction of the first, causing it to falter and weave to one side. This was the first glimpse Jack had that there were actual witches present - for it had all appeared as a projection at that point.

Then he got the message from Cleath, direct in his mind, "throw a net high above the hunter - throw it to pass over his head, NOW!"

So he does, he reaches into his bag, takes a net, and throws it like he had been taught by Pherial. First, he spins it in his hands over his head, like spinning a pizza base, then lift and throw. Its centripetal force gave it shape and created a gyroscope. They had explained, the spinning copper net interacted with the electric fields, slicing the psychic bonds being generated and creating a faraday cage effect. Little did he suspect he would have caught anything, but somehow a thing (he didn't know what to call the formless, writhing creatures) landed in his net. Pure luck.

Another salvo from the one who had been forced to duck, this time Cleath spun a net, and held it there as a sort of shield. The psychic waves buffeted and distorted it, but it held. "Not what I imagined witch hunting would be like," Jack muttered to himself.

The real hunters laughed, "This is sport, Brother Jack!" Pherial called out, once more his booming voice disorientating the attacking creatures. This is when they started the singing, beginning with the old sea shanty, *"Soon may the Wellerman come."* Pherial sang out the song in a rich bass. The pair joined in to the well-known and loved song.

Soon may the Wellerman come
To bring us sugar and tea and rum
One day, when the tonguin' is done
We'll take our leave and go

There once was a ship that put to sea
The name of the ship was the Billy of Tea
The winds blew up, her bow dipped down
O blow, my bully boys, blow

Soon may the Wellerman come
To bring us sugar and tea and rum
One day, when the tonguin' is done
We'll take our leave and go

She had not been two weeks from shore
When down on her a right whale bore
The captain called all hands and swore
He'd take that whale in tow

Soon may the Wellerman come
To bring us sugar and tea and rum
One day, when the tonguin' is done
We'll take our leave and go

Before the boat had hit the water
The whale's tail came up and caught her

All hands to the side, harpooned and fought her
When she dived down low

Soon may the Wellerman come
To bring us sugar and tea and rum
One day, when the tonguin' is done
We'll take our leave and go

Jack could feel the difference as they sang - the words flowed out with a hearty goodness, repelling the energy of the witches. It formed a bubble over them, a resonant barrier that seemed impervious to their threat. It drew a harmonic from Giza and amplified it, their harmony forming a harmonic bridge that held the power of the witches at bay

But just when they thought the task was done, just as they started to relax, a very different energy came onto the field - masculine, not feminine. A thing no one had ever dealt with before. It took the form of a fiery dragon, sending out acid and cruel imaginings. Venomous hatred clawed the air giving it a metallic taint.

"A real life DRAGON?" Cleath had an enormous curiosity, so great that broke through its bitterness. "That is amazing!" he exclaimed, apparently not noticing the threat it posed. "And so beautiful, look, golden scales - what a treasure we have found."

Pherial had been very much on the back foot with this last assault, it was like nothing they had ever experienced. The gusto of their sea shanty had dissipated as the sour cynicism of thought from this creature burned the air. "Aye, it is beautiful young one," he said, peering through the mist. His thoughts were more that this was the sour voice of the choir, the lone, bitter harpy that nagged, the true reason he never married, the mother of misery he had to bear for a decade while his father rotted. This was the reason he hated the witches so damn much. But the pure hearted Cleath kept his misery from submerging him.

Then the tide began to shift. The mist parted and maybe one hundred yards away, a golden snake-like creature with legs unfurled its wings, to display its true magnificence.

Without any hesitation, the boy starts on a song Jack didn't even know he knew - how could he? There were no churches in the new world, no hymn singing, yet out from his heart flowed an ancient song. Had he in some way plucked it from his OWN thoughts? Yet what he sang was true! The first thought from his consciousness was one of an amazed shock, that from this gloom something so stunning could have emerged.

The boy sang the first chorus perfectly, his high soprano voice cutting through the air like sunlight. Nay, it WAS sunlight. His joyous nature, his heart of gold itself started to ring, as he praised the dragon before him.

All things bright and beautiful
All creatures great and small
All things wise and wonderful
'Twas God that made them all

It seems so natural that Jack's baritone would join him on the second verse. He remembered his grandmother, before the fall, when they would go to church. He had been bored with the religion, but the singing was beautiful. The mother that died had seemed less of a burden, the father than wasn't there less important. Singing in his grandmother's church, he had felt free. He joined the second verse.

Each little flower that opens
Each little bird that sings
He made their glowing colors
And made their tiny wings

Now Pherial had his composure back. Cleath must have sent the words to his mind, for he too joined, his rich bass filling out the song. A resounding harmonic pushed aside the doubts and fears, ringing out like a hammer striking the anvil to make a perfect sword.

All things bright and beautiful
All creatures great and small
All things wise and wonderful
'Twas God that made them all

The three-part harmony flowed out, defiant against all that resisted their song, it was seeping through the cracks in the darkness, bringing light, peace, and a certainty of presence. They were about to start on the fourth verse when abruptly a voice cut them short.

"Enough!" exclaimed a powerful magnetism. It was not a voice as much as a demanding whisper inside your brain, but they felt the word as a finality. "This contest is DONE!"

There was a squealing of pain as the mists started to part, revealing sunlight that poured down to cleanse the land of its sins. Jack called out, "You will surrender the Blessed Isles!" he demanded.

Then a quiet acceptance, "Done," the dragon seemed to say, before wheeling around and taking to the sky. And then, stillness. Where there had been a raging surge of harmonics and energy, now there was nothing.

"Well, that was a surprise," laughed Pherial.

"THAT was meant to be our death," commented Jack bitterly. He had suspected a subterfuge, a reason why they so readily agreed to this battle. It was why he had worked so hard to extract the word the Ethereals used for Britain, thinking they would reveal some other area, claiming this is what they thought he meant. He had never suspected they had mythical creatures of flesh and blood, like this dragon. *Why did it not just kill them*, he wondered.

It is a thing of beauty, Cleath whispered into their minds. *Where one soul sees Satan, another sees God. Where one heart feels love, another in the same story feels bitterness. This is such a one that sees purely what IS. We were seen to be worthy.*

"Worthy of what?" Jack was relieved, but he could not shake the impression of that thing flying over and squashing them. No net, no coin, nothing but a subatomic Lazer was cutting that monster down. Which was when, above him, he heard the whisper of the anti-gravs. GOOD, perhaps his insurance policy had paid off.

The two-way crackled. "Confirmed boss, the ionic soup is rolling back from Britain as we speak. Seems like you won. What the fuck was that golden thing?"

Jack picked up and pressed the button, "Merry meet Cliff," he jested in the old English. "THAT my friend was a DRAGON, a real life fucking DRAGON. And I suspect the ionic cannon on your ship is what decided our fate, not his good graces." He looked at Cleath, who had a Mona Lisa smile. "That and the fact Cleath here softened him up with straight out flattery."

He stood there, wondering for a long moment if the Dragon was not a more manageable asset than the child. Cleath looked directly up at him, straight into his heart. The boy could stop it, if he wished, Jack knew, as did Cleath. "Do you understand the risk you pose to ALL of us?" he asked directly.

The boy just smiled, sweetly, his young face belying the power in the brain behind it. "The world still needs us." A long moment of peering into his soul, then the haunting old song, *"It's a strange, strange world we live in, Master Jack."*

THAT was his answer? a curious song from the 1970's from a virtually unknown band? He was an obtuse creature - Yet the fact remained, just as the young fellow had proven what he could do, he also proved how great a threat he was. If he demonstrated this power to those back in London, he also showed them a reason for them to fear him. And how could Jack respond? "Stay in his good graces then!" Because THIS was the only message he could impart. Soon enough they would consider Cleath to be a greater threat than the witches.

This meant that the freeing of the ionic soup from Britain, must be attributed solely to Pherial Artrim. This child needed to remain a secret.

As if understanding where his thoughts were going, Cleath said. "We must turn up the power of the Morrigan. Drive the mist back another fifty miles. The message must be certain and clear. These, as you have seen, are creatures of power, and they only understand and respect power." Then he paused, doing that sideways tilt of the head that the witches would do when faced with a coin, "Do you imagine they are not seeking to retrieve this power, even now, in the minds of your fellows? Do you wonder why the witches gave back their Blessed Isles? It is because they are already inside the minds of many on your ship."

Jack got the message loud and clear. "Cliff, drop down and take us back to the outpost. You got recordings of everything?"

"I have them, Boss," he almost smiled.

"Get them off to Bladwell, marked top secret. We don't need the others seeing how this went down. The mist rolling back is proof enough of the program." he replied. This was the most sensible path, reveal as little as needed, and let them believe it was Pherial who did it. They will accept this as he was the man in charge. He looked down at the little parcel of TNT beside him and sent him the clear message. *No one must suspect what you are capable of.*

"Only a matter of time," answered Pherial, also tuned into their thoughts.

"We will cross that bridge when we need to build it," answered Jack. "So far we have only one person outside our immediate group understanding that Cleath here is a level Five. The rest believe he is a level Four, and for all our sakes, we need this charade to continue."

Cliff was all smiles as he landed the flitter in the now vacant sports arena. He looked about, "Remember when we would all go to a football game? That's what I miss most, a day out with mates, cheering your team. The new world is kind of dull in this way."

oooOOOOooo

Mark Bladwell looked at the council before him, pointing out the window at the bright, sunny day. "What proof do you need?" he demanded. "Here it is, all of Britain freed from the soup. The soil can now be rejuvenated without the need for magnetic bubbles, and rainfall is starting to happen with ocean convection kicking in. Leave Jack Blake and his people to do their thing, we will do ours."

Doubting faces glared at him, "We have invested a great deal in Blake, and he runs his own show with no gratitude at all for what we have done for him, supporting him all these years. I say they should be based back here, where we can see what they are doing." Midge Fulton was the small-minded bureaucrat controlled by his minders in the academic faction.

"Speaking of gratitude," Bladwell went over and opened up a window. "How long since you were free to open a window and breath fresh air? Don't hand me that crap, I am in charge of the project, not you, and if you want to argue I will just shut it all down. Is that what you want?"

It was a question of jurisdiction, and the controlling political wing of the academics desperately wanted to pull the witch project, as it was known, under their wing. "We supplied the team that gave Blake his breakthrough. We can recall them just as easily!" Fulton threatened.

Bladwell laughs, "Ok, then - little Hitlers all let us rejoice! Recall them, do it! Stop these petty threats. But do you imagine it is possible that the scientists you claim YOU sent, the ones hand-picked by Blake, might possibly ignore you? Then where would you be? No ears, no eyes, no clue - Not so different from now, really."

The mining faction was now firmly on his side, while the political faction was not going to go against him with the current success. It meant Bladwell could afford to ridicule the academics - a thing he took great pleasure in. "But today I am here not about the Witch Project, but a new suggestion, a worthy one we can seriously consider now the air is clear - The miners want to bring back FOOTBALL, gentlemen, and the politicians and academics have been invited to form a team.

He laughed inwardly as the attitude changed from abrasion to interest. Jack was right again.

But one lone voice stood up, ignoring the suggestion, Professor Hargraves, the head of the Academic Faction. "What is required by government regulation is to have a telepath on board. Now, I believe we have one at Blake's outpost, a level four? We must have regulation complied with, so bring the level four back here, thank you."

Ah, the real reason for this meeting, they want to strip the core of power out of Jack's team. "As you all know, we have designated London a ship, for the purpose of meeting our onboard charter. Accordingly, I have this day designated Jack Blake's outpost as a ship, which HAS met regulation and has a telepath on board. So, I would suggest that if you want one, you either resurrect the dead guy or find another. The boy is essential to the team, you all know that, and I won't be allowing you to destroy the one chance we have of rebuilding this planet. Any other questions?"

"What is this so-called ship called!" demanded Hargraves.

"The Cairo," Bladwell laughed. "As you would know, the city of Cairo was named after the Ancient Greek word, Keiros, a place of opportunity. From the strict regulation of TIME, Chronos, we emerge into the moment, the point of opportunity, that which we call the Keiros. This is what this new ship represents, gentlemen, opportunity. One that will not be ruined by the petty bureaucrats and academics."

With this, he walked from the council room, stamping his authority once more on their bleating hearts. They hated him, they hated the power he had attained, but they could do nothing. The miners were in his camp, and with the air and ground cleared up, they could consider real sports once more. That meant meeting the miners head-on in a football game, where the miners would most certainly win.

Jack was right, had been all along. The real threat to Earth were these tired old fools, desperate for power regardless of the cost to their own people. Next, the meeting he WOULD enjoy, seeing the men and letting them know that the ship Cairo was now a registered port of call. What this meant under the regulations was that they could go there for a drink, enjoy the view, and if any pretty locals happen to walk in - well, there you go.

Later that day, with all meetings done and the roaring cheers of the miners still ringing in his ears, he had Jack up on a screen. The old man was looking very old - not much time left, Bladwell would have guessed. "As you expected, they tried to draught Cleath. They have no way around the registration of the outpost as the good ship Cairo. Which I have also designated a port of call, so expect some woman hungry miners to be turning up."

Jack was tired but pleased. "Bladwell, you have saved the whole damn show here."

"You gave us Britain, Jack. It was the least I could do. What is the program moving forward?"

"It is hard deciphering what these witches want or how they think, seems to be they want a yearly contest. Which could be a problem, as I don't know how much longer Pherial and myself have."

"I am authorizing a rejuvenation clinic for the good ship Cairo. It will give you both a few more years. Once a year is slow, but from what I saw of the footage, these creatures play for keeps. What was the dragon thing?"

"As far as I can tell, it was a real fucking dragon - straight out of a fantasy novel. Not mist, not generated - real - I sense that these are the things that really run the show. They/it/them/he controls the witches, the witches control everything else."

Bladwell looked once more at the holographics. "Could it be some sort of hologram? Yes, it looks substantial and real, but as this is nothing like anything else we have seen in the mist, maybe they have found an old world unit - they were common in cinemas. Maybe they managed to master holographic projection?"

Jack considered this for a long moment. His pale blue eyes seemed just a little more bleached, the skin under them, just a little more tired. Age was bearing down, and he knew it. "The presence was male. All the witches give a female sense, or so Pherial tells me. He was very convinced the dragon was real and he is not easily fooled. What I am postulating, and which Cleath agrees with, is that the mist is like a dividing line between their world and ours. For some reason, what lives there is unable to come into our world, just as we can't go into theirs - but for a moment one pushed all the way into the mist. This is all just guesswork - did you show the footage to anyone?"

"Good God no, that would be like setting fireworks off in the gunpowder factory. Those useless creatures that call themselves scientists would be over there in droves, looking for evidence to write new theories. We have a world to save, not curiosity to feed." Mark reached to the icebox and pulled out a beer, tilting it towards Jack as a sort of 'cheers', then took a long draught.

Jack turned to look off-camera, and waved someone over, "Pherial, you need to speak with Bladwell."

The camera swung over to the witch hunter, "Master Mark?" he asked.

Bladwell switched on the translator. "Brother Pherial, how goes your day?" Jack had coached him on how to speak with the locals.

"It is well, Brother Mark. Does your day travel well?"

"It has been long but rewarding, Brother Pherial. Long but rewarding...." he paused for the appropriate time for the nuance of greeting to be completed. "To your recent conquest, I salute the Gregorians. The dragon you found, tell me of it."

"Ah, Brother Mark, a magnificent thing. Great glowering eyes, full of malice and hate, contrasting the beautiful golden body. We sang it an ancient tune from the old world, a perfect three-part harmony, which seemed to be effective. Yet we could not kill it. I am not sure we can."

"Brother Jack says it is male and that you believe it to be real, not an Ethereal? How would you come to this conclusion?"

Pherial smiled, showing the perfect teeth behind the weather beaten old face. "That it was real, or that it was male, Brother Mark?"

"Both."

"Well, the first mistake most will make is thinking that because a witch appears as mist, that she is not real. She is mist until she is plugged with a coin, then the mist dissipates, and for a short time, the physical form of a sad woman is revealed. I have the view that the mist is a projection, a sort of armor they wear. As to knowing if she is a woman, it is clear when you see the dying body. This dragon needed no such mist - and as to it being male, well, this is a thing you just know."

Bladwell considered this for a long moment. A sort of inter-dimensional breach formed the opening for the mist to come through. They had cleared the ionosphere of the toxin, but clearing the land was another matter. An intuition snapped into place. "Thank you Brother Pherial. I must get back to Brother Jack now."

He switched off the translator, "Jack, these things, whatever they will prove to be, appear to be controlled by harmonics. THIS has to be able to be measured as a quantum. In fact, the mist itself has to be able to be regulated and measured as a quantum."

"And how does this help us?" Jack is curious.

"If I can write accurate equations up, based on the data from your battle, and feed them into our quantum computers, they will be able to analyze and predict fluctuations, to the extent we may be able to take the control of the mist away from them. We pretty much did this with the ionosphere, worked out the pattern of resonance, and used radionics to disperse it, but the ground radiation seemed to be tied to a more complex and resilient energy field."

"You thinking something like a Tesla Tower?" Jack and every engineer in the 24th century had studied the math of Tesla. If what Mark said was true about being able to run equations at a quantum level, it was possible. "Set to run a predictive on the flux the generates the mist and counter it to settle the phase to zero, this what you mean?"

"Exactly, flatten the peaks that sharpen the ionic resonance. That should reduce it to sum zero, no more mist. We can walk in their world and see what THEY see - and maybe grab the portal machinery that lets them in here."

"Plus, no need to expose our level Five," Jack was liking having his erstwhile sparring partner, the man who usually countered his arguments as a devil's advocate, on side. Then a thought, "Could you create something portable, a thing we can carry in with us to our next battle?"

Bladwell has the image in his head, a sort of vest with five reference nodes. "I will get to work on it," he answered. "But thinking about it, the witches obviously have a way of switching off the resonance that creates the mist. My question is more, will it be necessary to do the battle thing, putting us at risk, when we might be able to copy their technology and reverse it. It's a thought I have been having, just as we use resonance to roll back the mist, perhaps they use similar to roll it forward?"

Jack scratched an ear, "Feels strange having you onside, Bladwell. Yeah, I am not a tech and what you say makes sense. What I am not sure is what you are suggesting, because with a vest I start to think of … "

Bladwell interrupted. "I didn't mention a vest, Jack - I got the image of one, but never said that."

They looked at each other, "Cleath, I suppose." Jack laughed. "You want to show yourself young fella?"

The boy comes into view. *DAMN*, thought Bladwell. *He can make himself invisible to ELECTRONIC equipment as well?* "Did you put the image of a five-point resonance vest into my thoughts, Cleath?"

"Not really, Master Bladwell. I saw it, my witch showed it to me, she calls it a 'Wesech'. The use of the blue stone, Lapis Lazuri, with gold creates an energy the mind can use and direct."

Bladwell references his computer and flashes up an image of the odd collar the Pharaohs of Egypt used to wear. "You mean, you saw something like one of these?"

The boy nods.

Not exactly a vest, but the idea was the same. Bladwell's mind is now racing forward - Lapis Lazuli was the most curious gemstone, dielectric yet loaded with semiconducting pyrite grains. People mistake the pyrite for gold, but it is 'fools gold', which is a semiconductor. The stone was also diamagnetic, despite having grains of iron. The thing was, in effect, nature's transistor. One thing a mining company executive understood, the properties of valuable stones. "I will get a team onto it - the clue of Lapis may be exactly what we need in selecting a frequency. I am thinking what we might be able to achieve is a sort of key that lets you into THEIR dimension."

Jack gets where he is going, "Just like they sent a giant from their world into our, to steal the Morrigan, we can go there and take what THEY are using to come into our world. That seems high risk, but better than waiting a year for them to set up another trap." *Or build another set of pyramids, and keep them in check,* he thought.

"Cleath, why does your witch tell us these things? Do you know?" Bladwell is curious. He can sense no deception in the child, but perhaps he is bait. Perhaps they have done a judo move, and are using their strengths against them.

"I do not believe she even understands why herself, Master Mark. I do not compel her, though I could. I did not even ask for this, though I confess, I have been wondering what their side of the coin, so to speak, is like." Cleath was, as always, an open book.

Bladwell signed off, assigning a team to develop the concept of an ionic vest based on an ancient Egyptian design. He had a nudge after earlier discussion with Blake that there was more to the Pharaoh thing than met the eye, and on the mans recommendation, he had read the "Far Memory" books of Joan Grant. It seemed to him that the jewelry of the Egyptians acted as a sort of psychic amplifier, not just as decoration. Perhaps it was ALL part of a program to keep the witches on their side of the fence.

But he could not shake the suspicion that Cleath was in some way being handled by his personal witch. He understood the concept, you dominated your opponent, they became your slave, your chattel. But she DIED. Unless, of course, the body of the witch this side of the barrier was a sort of avatar - a thing created to exist outside of their own dimension. In which case, she was alive and well, and doing everything she could to get him to their side of the equation.

While HE was thinking of ways to get over to their dimension, they may be secretly organizing it, just to get their hands of the level Five telepath. It was a razor's edge.

A Song in Their Hearts

Ciera and Chara laughed as they worked the soils. They were happy to be farmers again, working happily with with family and friends, having completed the greatest task of their generation. They had kept faith, been true, and believed in the Morrigan. Even so, witnessing her almighty power still left them breathless. Truly they were blessed.

But even more so, for Master Jack had arranged for some old tech he had found to be presented to his village, in honor of the services given by his clan. A machine that was unruly, poorly disciplined, and wild, but once harnessed a gift from the gods themselves. A sun-powered tractor, Master Jack called it - a machine that dug the earth, slashed the fields, and harvested the crops. It did the work of a hundred men, giving more time for song and laughter.

It was a tricky beast, and they had been warned it could bite, so great care had to be taken. "It is an old age machine," Master Jack had explained. "The Sun herself powers it. She is old but reliable, while you must add on the implements for the job you wish to do." Where he then showed them how to add the orbital hoe for plowing, the slasher for clearing, and the harvester for cropping. "You will still have to pick the fruit trees by hand, but for most of your grains and legumes, this will make life a lot easier."

Ciera did not protest or claim they were unworthy. As head of the clan now, he had learned much of leadership, and the grateful acceptance of gifts. He knew they had earned the right, while the pride of his people in the job well done was worthy of song. And the new songs they now sang were joyous, a thing that they had been taught called Sea Shanties. All the harvesting crews would swing to the infectious rhythm as they did their daily work.

The Morrigan protected them. The incidents of Whytes stealing children or animals had fallen to almost zero. The mist had dropped back over a hundred miles, and clans were vying for the right to harvest the new fields. While the sun healed the lands his clan had taken a large tract close to the mist - so close they could reach it in but an hours walk. This had been a place of fear, but no longer. The Morrigan blessed and protected them.

The arrangements with the new lands were very simple, 30% of all they harvested were placed as land tax near the place of the Tor, where a special building had been erected. And with the sun tractors provided by

Master Jack, they did not need to move a whole village. Instead, a select band from each clan was sent to live in the village near the Tor. Already Chara had met a future wife, no doubt part of the reason for his permanent smile.

"What a joy and blessing it is to work under the watchful eye of the Morrigan," Chara sighed as they finished the days labor. Though you could barely call it work, the tractor did all that, they just guided its wilful heart.

"Not a day or an hour passes without an offering of thanks from my heart," replied Ciera. It was true, they had a blissful, rich life now. It wasn't just the easy work and comfortable homes in which they now lived, it was the vibrant, enthralling connections they were making with all the other clans at the village each night.

At the tavern, they would drink and sing the songs of the great dragon hunt, a thing of immeasurable beauty that faced the Master Artrim. Already he had beaten three Twitches when the golden beast arrived, yet despite the odds against them, with courage and wits, he and his small band sang the beast to sleep. It was a wonderful song. A song of all that mattered: courage, defying the odds, and rising to the challenge.

Later that evening, as they ate their shared meal with the other workers back at the tavern, cheering the day and downing some ales, the head of the Theirn clan came to speak with them. "Ho there Marth, what news?"

He bowed acknowledgment to the leader of the great task, "Ho Ciera, Chara, I was wondering if you could confirm what I have heard." He paused, Ciera gave his assent to hear more. "As you know, our messenger passes the outpost on the way here with news of the clan. He tells me that when he called in, one of our women was speaking with a foreigner, on friendly terms. He went to make certain she was good, and while he was talking, the man asked the messenger if he knew who were the ones going to the new lands, the place called Britain. Do you know of this?"

There had been more than a few foreigners at the outpost, and their women were attracted to them, which caused a degree of jealousy. Their own clan was far from the place, and they had none of their people there. "Master Jack had mentioned that the great effort by Master Artrim had been so powerful, lands had cleared across the waters. There could be truth to it, Marth. I expect we will see the Old Man soon enough and can ask him directly."

"It gnaws at the Soul of the elders, that the young could leave the tribe for new lands," he explained.

"Does it then bother your old folk that you and yours are here, working at the Tor?"

He sighed, "I suppose you are correct - distance is distance. But the thought of a strange land, with a new people, it frightens many."

Ciera agreed, "This is true. Change IS a thing that can cause fear. The unknown is a journey only the brave may take, and the old are more than willing to turn their heads away from the shifting sands, to pretend they don't exist. But we both know, change comes. Look at the lands around the Tor - once barren, controlled by witches, now bountiful and rich. The threat of change may cause some of your people to fear, yet at the same time, the promise of change will provide those with courage the opportunity and enterprise they need to better their lives."

Chara slapped Marth on the back, "See old friend! We undertook the great challenge for the future of our children! How can we then turn and refuse them the future we fought so hard to attain?"

"Well met," Marth was smiling now. The words were true, they lifted the fog of concern from his brow. "But what message do you recommend I send back to the elders?"

Ciera shook his head, "It is not for me to come between you and yours, Marth. Here in the folds of the Morrigan, I am sure she will whisper you the words they need to hear. But if I were to think of anything, it would be trust. As they say in the scripture: *Trust in the path as it unfolds, be certain of your step, find your way in the darkness with the light of courage in your heart*."

"The words are true," Marth responded, lifting his ale to salute the two that carried the team forward, the pair who showed them the way to complete the great task. "Now it is time for song!" And with this, Marth started out with one of the new Sea Shanties the people had all grown to love. Soon all were singing in praise of the Morrigan and the joy she had brought them.

ooo0000ooo

Professor Eric Hargraves sat in the room with several scientists and Midge Fulton. "We know they are up to something, but there is very little we can do to put pressure on while they have the miners on side." Midge was explaining to his masters. He had sold out long ago, even before the return to Earth. He was in the admin for the ship and had been organizing special privileges for the scientists since the start of the tour. Technically, he was in charge of the security of technical and academic staff when they were off ship on some world. In reality, he had no role once they were back on Earth, none of them did.

No one was signing paychecks because the company that employed them had shut down long ago, and the banking systems where the funds had gone were defunct. That was the hard part to hang a hat on, none of them had any purpose under law, nor any role. Day-to-day decisions were based on what was seen as necessary for long-term survival. Even so, the scientists had pretty much tied up the political wing and had been in charge until this latest fiasco.

Now, all the power Hargraves had nurtured on their long years on this planet had been eroded by that archaeologist. ALL their power had been subsumed by his camp and Bladwell. But, this scientific development that Blake and Bladwell wanted, that was THEIR business - this vest idea was based on a sound theory, and the notion of being able to traverse into the witch dimension was like putting cheese in front of mice. It had their plasma engineers and quantum mechanics agog with possibility - REAL science, in real world application.

"Well, they need us now, Fulton. We need to milk it for everything it is worth. Gain concessions, get us access to the cross-over site and get us IN on one of the expeditions. These are my requirements if they want us to help them out." Hargraves was intent on infiltrating the little world Bladwell had created since the telepath turned up. "They are hiding shyte, we all know it, and soon enough Blake will find some excuse to get us evicted from any influence at all."

Midge Fulton pointed out the obvious. "Bladwell has changed, he is now running defense for Blake. He has the miners in his pocket and the Admin will not go against them, not openly at least. I don't see a way to pull this back, not after he walked the damn walk and cleared all of Britain." What he was thinking was: *Might be time to switch allegiance.*

"Blake will stuff this country with his Arabs, ignorant savages. It is the ultimate power grab, he will get them into the voting block and give himself total control. It has to be his game plan."

Fulton laughed, "That's just stupid - The guy is hitting a hundred and ten. The best he has is ten more years and are you telling me an old man is so desperate for power he would change our whole system? The guy won, against all the odds, against all the opposition over the years, he did what we couldn't do - He fed us, he organized furs, and gave us linen from flax. Time to give up the vendetta Hargraves. He has WON."

"You are forgetting one important detail - all this happened since he discovered his little telepath. We had him, Fulton - We had him tied up and in OUR court, then all of a sudden a miracle! A telepath comes and everything flips. Well, I am not buying it - We all know what a telepath can do, and you can bet your bootstraps this one is pulling Blake's strings and getting his people over here. The real question is what do they want?"

"Give it up, Eric. They are primitive farmers with little notion we even existed, let alone a mysterious power-hungry creature suddenly taking over minds and making a power grab."

"Idiot, what is owning the telepath? I say it is the witches. This is their plot to get people they can control over here, to take charge of the last of humanity. They want our tech, then they will evict us." Eric Hargraves was an old bigot, narrow-minded, and bitter. His pinched face betrayed years of hatred while his sharp nature and beady eyes demonstrated a total lack of empathy for those around him.

"Then why did they give back Britain? What you claim makes no logical sense, they already had it half-submerged in mist. No, Blake's brilliance at calculating the correct frequencies to push back the mist worked, despite your professional assessment opposing his plan. His gambit for going into battle for the British Isles is what gained our freedom from the mist. Eric, I am done here, with the academics and with you. I am going to wish Jack Blake and his crew the best of luck in clearing up the rest of the planet. If you had any sense, you would do the same." With this, Midge Fulton turned his back on a more than thirty-year association with the 'old guard', as everyone knew it.

He left the bitter old man behind. It was time to sever the links, they had failed, Blake had won, end of story. Hargrave's strange fiction of a telepath mysteriously being taken control of by the witches and somehow orchestrating this whole show was so far-fetched it beggared belief. Even so, because of the claim, he had to go through the verification process with the child, which annoyed him. It meant going out to that damn outpost and putting up with the smirk of Blake, knowing he had checkmated them all.

He patched through the verification request to Bladwell.

ooo0000ooo

"The logical question, what is the power supply?" Bladwell is distracted from his work with a message from Fulton. Just what he didn't need. The scientists in front of him had been vetted and held no connection to Hargraves and his people, he continued, "We have the sun, that is our power pack, they hate the sun it seems, so they have a different power source."

Mike Johnson, a plasma tech, puts up his hand, "Maybe they still use the sun? Just as high level UV creates Ozone because of pollutants, perhaps the sun reacts on the ionic soup that in some way powers up their systems. I can simulate conditions and see what sort of plasma evolves. It would be good to get something from there and see what sort of energy it absorbs."

Mark agrees, "Worth checking. Our bodies need sunlight to recharge ATP, so it is reasonable to assume they are absorbing SOMETHING, but what? Where does it come from? And WHY do they decompose in sunlight? I will ask if we can get a Whyte captured and brought here."

Pete Tolly, a physics engineer, a man who designed nano-tech motors, had a suggestion, "Maybe what we see as their body here in our dimension is just a mockup, a space suit of sorts. The sunlight strips the protective layer away and the physical form evaporates. I have been thinking a lot about this, maybe these things ARE energy, or maybe they have to switch to being energy to cross the barrier, but what they are NOT is physical matter as we know it."

Bladwell grunts, "So we all thought, but how did they create a physical giant to carry off the resonance generator? That was physical, but with the peculiar characteristic of being susceptible to sunlight. There must be a key with the toxicity of copper."

"It is an ionically active metal. But the fact it activates when in contact with an Ethereal WITHOUT a charge being supplied indicates that the copper is being charged by the creatures. They must carry a high static impedance. Burgel and Szuu published centuries ago how you can use this to generate intercellular spectro-analysis - Maybe they reverse this, and project this impedance, it might describe how they can 'see' but also why sunlight destroys them." Young Tom Flag was a brilliant biologist who specialized in morphic field analysis.

"This seems likely, Tom, but how do we engineer a similar sort of suit for US, one that allows us to go into THEIR world. Understanding how they come here is only half the picture we need to color in. We have been given a clue with Lapis Lazuli - WHY would that allow us to interact their environment?" Mark Bladwell asks in return.

"Easy one," said Tom, casually. "The combination of silica and pyrite in the stone, in conjunction with the gold it was always set with in with Egyptian jewelry, is like the crystal in the radio, it helps us tune into to the signal. Plus it is diamagnetic, and I am going to suggest that the Ethereals use a sort of magnetic pulse to regulate their energy supply - so the stone will disrupt that effect reaching us. It will create an ionic bubble, not dissimilar to how we use anti-static gloves."

"So field generation? Just as the harmonics in the resonator push back the influence, you can set up a sort of 'glove' around a person that allows them to walk in the mist frequency but not be touched by it? That is what we need, but it still doesn't explain how they create creatures that can walk in our world."

"I think it does, Bladwell," Tom Flag continued. "I will suggest that they grow them in the interim place, where they control the physical with the mist. These things still can't take direct sunlight, but perhaps they are a sort of lab rat, grown in the mist and more accessible to our world."

"Control the physical? Does this mean you think they are non-physical?" Phil Reaver asked, he was invested in the physics of dimensional cross-over.

"Not exactly, Phil," Tom stood up to address everyone. "The way I see this is that is is like tuning in to a radio - all the stations are there, all the time, beaming out the music - but you need a crystal that vibrates to that frequency to translate waves of energy into reality. Adjust the wavelength and you experience their reality, so to speak. I suspect they use the mist like we use the dial on a radio, tuning the frequency to align their physical presence with ours. Without it, they dissipate, but maybe that is just them leaving this dimension."

"Spectrographic analysis of the mist reveals it is just this - ionic mist." counters Phil Reaver.

"That's right - the mist is nothing. Radio waves are nothing. It is the INFORMATION that gets imprinted on them that is everything. The mist is a carrier wave, the proof is they cannot exist here without it. My suggestion is that we play with what polarities are charging up the mist, and develop our own way to re-tune them- technically this means we should be able to walk in their world."

There was a general agreement in the room that this was worth pursuing, and several of the scientists and engineers present started looking up charts and tests done on the mist in recent days, looking at the ionic fluctuation.

Mark Bladwell picked up a small bell and rang it, calling for silence, then looked at the men and women before him, "I know some of you are going against your own faction to do this work - but this is not about miners versus scientists. It is about cleansing the world of the mist and defeating the witches."

He looked at them, they all seemed OK. "First step, we need to be certain that the mist is a result of field generation. Second: We then need to be able to direct it, so we can reverse it. We know this can happen because the Witches have PROVEN it can be reversed, Britain is clear.

"Third: We then need equipment that can allow our people to cross into THEIR world and take the fucking thing that is pouring the mist into ours. OUR world, people! Fourth: Remember one simple thing in all you do: This is OUR planet, we want it back."

As he left the meeting he read the note sent by Fulton, a request to test the telepathy candidate. He dialed him up, "So what NOW Fulton? What other little concocted notion have you got to interfere with our plans to save the world?"

Midge doesn't blame Mark for his hostility, "Bladwell, I have severed ties with Hargraves. Blake has won, but Hargraves did put up one specific red flag, the possibility that the telepath is in some way being controlled by the witches. It is a security question I am sure you have canvassed yourself, but to bring the political faction and the remaining doubters of the scientific faction onside, we will need to verify allegiance."

"Fulton, I have good Intel that a few from your crazy wing wants to kill the boy. I have no intention of allowing any of you near him."

"Mark, believe me on this. I have severed ties. Hargraves has gone off the deep end, yet his irrational hatred has some merit. You know this as much as I do, the boy even talks of speaking with his witch. We need independent testing, and with this in place and verified I can guarantee no more opposition. Without it, all you will get is opposition."

Bladwell openly laughed, "Is that a promise or a threat? And frankly, it is not much of either. We are doing fine without you lot, in fact, probably a lot better because your absurd and stupid short-sightedness is no longer a hindrance."

There was a period of silence on the other end of the line. "Yeah, well I deserved that I guess. Mark, you hold all the cards, but the facts are, Blake is old, very old. He could be dead tomorrow, and where will we all be? The telepath is very much connected to him and you KNOW what can happen when they suffer loss or a loved one dies. I am given to understand that the two people he most identifies with are Blake and the witch hunter, this Artrim fellow - both very, very old."

"Mitch, I know, believe me I understand. This is why I authorized a regen plant for them at the outpost. And don't think I am not worried about exactly what you are saying, but verifying the lad who is already verified isn't going to change anything. I have seen him often, he is much more than just a kid with extraordinary talent, he is also a decent, sweet little guy. I very much doubt the witch would even know HOW to act that way - I am certain he is not under their control."

"Yet, if for some reason he is, if even a small percentage of him is under control, even when he is sleeping, you know a telepath can cause the death of a person they perceive as a threat. He may not even be aware consciously what he is doing, but Artrim and Blake might die in their sleep. THEN what happens? You know we can install a mind lock on certain frequencies, and you know it is normal practice to lock telepaths less they become a risk."

Bladwell listened to the reasoned voice, "Yes, your old ways of doing things stopped our last telepath from killing others, but it also made him feel helpless and depressed. I consider it likely your mind lock is what sent him into suicide mode. He was blaming the witches when what really happened was your conditioning stopped him expressing his natural urges."

He had to dance through this. Full assessment would reveal what the little guy actually was, and then they would all freak. "You know what the real problem is? A lack of trust. The people out there in Egypt consider trust, integrity, and honesty are the basis of all true society. They do not hesitate to trust each other. Their existence is based on believing in each other, so how do you think it will go down, you turning up full of distrust, asking to inspect his brain?"

Fulton seemed confused and objected. "It is simply procedure."

"Procedure in YOUR world where distrust is the norm. Telepaths could redirect gold shipments by controlling a mind, that sort of thing. They were needed but had to be regulated. Plus, you had to be sure they weren't bribed AND you had to stick them in an isolation room, then tell them it was for THEIR sake. It was very fooked up how you treated them. This little kid is still a kid, and I want him to stay that way as long as possible."

"So you expect us just to trust?"

"I expect you lot to do nothing, as you have always done. The ONLY person who has achieved anything significant in this place is the person YOU were convinced needed to be collared and controlled. Just like you want to do to the telepath. I thought the same for almost thirty years, but when I just went along with Jack Blake, look what fookin happened!" Bladwell wanted to shout, but he contained himself. "What happened is we finally started to get in charge of this planet again. Let's face it, if you people had won the day, we would have pumped on to a different habitable planet and started again. Remember who recommended that? Hargraves."

"To be fair, that was before we found a way to get the sunlight through. It wasn't looking positive back then, nor did we know if the scoop concept would work." Fulton protested.

"Look Mitch, I don't want or need an argument with you, or anyone. The fact is, we are the last remnants of the human race, billions are gone - dead. We have a wasteland of a planet, but with everyone working together, somehow we are rebuilding. Up to this point our existence here has been as a matter of survival. But in this last month we have made serious inroads towards proper expansion and ALL of it has wrapped around this remarkable little guy who popped out of nowhere." Time to switch gears and massage a little.

"Cleath is the reason we were able to talk to the Ethereals. He is the focal point for all discussions, all agreements, and is the core reason WHY we were able to gain of all of Britain in a matter of hours. We spent over sixty years reclaiming a few square miles - and even then it had to live under a magnetic dome. To have you lot upsetting the delicate balancing act Jack Blake is performing just cannot be allowed, end of story. That little boy is barely out of the blocks of puberty, let alone adjusted to an entire society that would be anathema to his sensibilities. You don't get this, and I know it sounds like an insult, but mentally, you stink. Your thinking, your way of seeing the world? To a telepath like Cleath, you are a dog that has just shat in the room. Nothing personal, but all your baggage, all your distrust, political maneuvering, and social conditioning makes you a very poor candidate to have ANY dealings with our boy." What Bladwell wanted to shout was, *"And if you try, he is a FIVE and will blow your little circuits!"* but he didn't.

There was a pause at the end of the phone. "While I am trying to understand exactly what all this personal abuse might mean, Bladwell, am I to presume that you will object to any application for verification assessment?"

"Not at all Mitch, I don't object to it at all, and indeed would far prefer things went by the book. What I object to is you and yours seeking to put the entire planet at risk because of your lack of comprehension of how important and how delicate our situation with the telepath is. The fact that YOU are so clueless is proof that you are not capable, and I think you will find if you insist on any such interference, the miners, the ones who DO understand a little of what is going on because they are happily chatting up the local girls at the good ship Cairo, may just take you out and give you an education."

"Is that a threat?"

"No, Mitch - you can consider it a promise. Anyone or anything turning up at the outpost without my express permission will be classed as a level three risk. All miners know and understand that the eradication of a level three is a priority, and further, actions taken to terminate a level three have no legal ramifications or consequences."

"But that is the equivalence of saying we are a threat to the entire expedition!" he exclaimed.

"Correct Mitch, you are. You fuck up our telepath and all this grinds to a halt. I won't let it happen and I have the legal authority and more importantly, the will, to ensure it doesn't."

Fulton signed off, saying he will consider it.

Bladwell sighed, for a minute he thought the guy was coming onside. Maybe he WAS genuine, that he had broken ranks with Hargraves. But as soon as that lot realized what they had on their hands with Cleath, their fear would seep out and start to poison the entire base. The men going over there were no problem, miners were simple folk - they wanted to work, fuck, and drink. That was normal to an uneducated tribal kid like Cleath, something he could understand. But people turning up to program your mind, instilling little blocks to make themselves feel safe, he would rebel. How, Bladwell had no idea, but the boy would object.

And maybe they didn't quite grasp, this kid was trained to kill witches, creatures that tried to get inside your mind and get you to do what they wanted you to. He had to keep the lad away from them at all costs, for all their sakes.

The New Pharaoh

The Outpost hummed with activity - the first example of the new gear to allow them entry into the witches' world had arrived and needed to be tested in the field. Tom Flag, the laconic blue-eyed blonde with the brilliant grasp of dimensional physics was chatting away with Jack Blake, explaining the principles.

"So, basically we insulate ourselves from their world, putting us into a sort of bubble?" Jack asked.

"Pretty much, the suit still has issues with stability, as the thing is generated by external current. It is ACTIVATED by the mist, and is essentially passive electronics, gaining its charge from both movement in, and interaction with, an ionic environment. We are being powered up by THEIR environment, in other words. If that is variable, the result we experience will be likewise." Tom leaned back, enjoying the magnificent view from the dam, sucking on a cold beer. "I can see why you wanted to stay here for so long, Jack."

If he were surprised when a teenage boy appeared in front of him, he didn't show it. "Will we be able to interact with their environment as well?" Cleath asked.

"Hey, the telepath! Hya kiddo, great to see you are interested. Yeah, you should be able to deal with their world in the same way we walk and talk in this one. Don't know for sure, but that is the plan."

Cleath smiled. Tom felt an intense warmth flow over his skin. He glanced up to Jack, knowing their last telepath had little by way of empathy, and even less by way of friendliness. "This is Cleath, Tom - he is the reason we are all here today. You may have noticed he is not like other telepaths, as in friendly, and we would like to keep things that way. So the less said about him back at the ship, the better."

The boy was looking intently at the young scientist, then with a surprised look, proclaims, "He is a telepath as well!"

Jack smiled and picked up the little guy. He needed constant touching and earthing, to balance out his energies, and to make sure he understood he was loved. "Yeah Cleath, there are a few of us who come from old tribes and keep a sense of our early tribal practice." Looking at Tom, he explained, "We two can walk a little in alternative dimensions naturally, which is all telepathy is, but this one is different - He can ALTER the dimension in which he walks."

"You kidding me?" Tom is astonished.

Jack hands him over the stats. He had known Tom for many years and was well pleased when he cracked the concept of a suit that could walk between the worlds. It was time to start educating the fellow in what they had with young Cleath.

"Whoa, and Bladwell knows this? Of course he does. No wonder he kept the bulk of people out. Hey kiddo, you know what all these figures mean?"

Cleath looked back blankly.

"Course you don't. You are still a kid. Let me say, I am very glad you are on our side." He looks back at Jack. "How long do you intend to keep this secret?"

Jack said little. He hadn't wanted to show him how Cleath was a Level Five, but Tom had to know the amount of power that the suits needed to be able to channel. He would need the stats to make it fully operational. "What I suggest is a small excursion to the fringe of the mist, to give these things a trial run."

Within the hour they were on the flitter traveling out to the far edges of their territory with Artrim and the full complement of witch hunters. Jack knew the moment they lit up the mist with this gear, it would be a flashing red light advertising their presence. He wanted in and out quickly to see what else they needed to do. He and Tom went on their own flitter, with Cliff as the pilot.

As they got underway, Jack explained, "You understand, we say nothing about Cleath when you get back?"

"I get why, have you explained the whole story to the little guy?"

"Hard to explain the taste of a banana. But it's not just the probes and the blocks, their fear and doubt will subjectively program our boy. It doesn't matter how clear and pure his mind is at the start, when you put a cucumber in a jar of pickles, soon enough you get just another pickle. Even if he resists, even if he blows them out of the water, the thousands of years of programming that runs their heads will get through. Memes are like that, they teach the young through signals, not through action. It is time for a new Earth, Tom - Our lot fucked up the last one. This is the new Eden, and Cleath is their Messiah."

Tom laughed, "As I recall, the Babylonian garden of creation had Lillith and Adon as the first humans, no snake. Lillith was the equal of man, but by the time the Judaic myth got written, she had turned into the snake, and Eve turns up as a subordinate. Just shows, one person's savior can be another's devil."

"We all just give him the love, help him where we can, and let him grow as he will. If they know they have a Five, they won't handle it, and we will have an all-out war on our hands. There is tremendous fear around telepathy, our own lack of control over our own minds is just part of it. The paradox is, of course, that they will create what they fear - to preserve their life, any telepath will take over the mind of a perceived threat. You can't press a trigger when someone is in your mind telling you not to. That is where the problem will start, and where it ends, who knows. The scientists and admin have control of the ship - They may just up stakes and leave, which is to no one's benefit."

"So, just nurse it through, leave them ignorant, and sort out the witches?"

Jack nods, "pretty much."

"And then?" Tom asks the obvious.

"Then, we see what we see," Jack replies.

Tom said nothing more but thought plenty. Jack was not unaware of what might happen but the simple truth was, he was not all that likely to see it. Everyone knew that telepaths were like racing horses, brilliant in a short run, but over time, they just got crazier and crazier. The blocks instilled were meant as a buffer to insanity for them and protection to the people around them.

He leaned back, one thing at a time. First, sort out the spacesuit, as he jokingly referred to the creations they were testing out today. "You know Jack," he said, "we all know about the garden of Eden, but have you considered the whole picture?"

Jack laughed, happy to have the subject changed. "What are you on about now?"

"Well, everyone blamed Satan for it all going pear-shaped, but think about it. Lucifer can't stand the strict rules of Heaven and bowing down to God isn't his thing. So he comes to Earth, plants a garden. Nice. Then there is a guy called Adam who turns up with his missus. They seem OK, but stupid, so Lucifer kindly offers them fruit from the tree of knowledge. Why? Maybe he wants to have a decent conversation, who knows.

"But bully boy God turns up and says: *No can do. I like my people dumb and stupid!* Worse, he throws a tantrum and boots everyone out of the garden. So who is the problem here? Satan was trying to help, but Mr. Rules has a big stick and says he was right and they were wrong.

"The whole lack of logic to all of it beggars belief. Why create a tree where the fruit was knowledge in the first place, then forbid it? Everyone knows forbidden fruit is the sweetest, everyone knows what human nature is like. God is supposed to be all-knowing and all kind, yet he puts a sure-to-fail test on the shoulders of his ignorant savages. THAT, my friend, is a sadist. If anyone you knew put some mice in a run, leaving the sweetest tasting fruit set into a trap that killed them, you would call them a sadist for sure.

"No, the snake was the good guy, trying to help the people out. God is the problem here." Tom laughed.

"And the hidden message is?" Jack questioned.

"No message and nothing hidden. Fact is, we all think we know what is right, but we only ever know half the story. Do you really think you can shut down the mist?"

"We have to - It wasn't reported, but Pherial and myself, left to our own devices, would be dead right now - or whatever happens when the witches get control of you. Cleath was the one who saved us, not with brilliant telepathic control, but downright admiration of what we faced." Jack pulled up a holo of the actual events.

"Fark," Tom whistles. "An actual dragon? They can bring in real life creatures to do their work? You can't combat that without serious firepower."

"Cliff was on standby to pull us out, not that hovers work all that well in the mist, but I also had an ionic cannon put on it, in case they tried something like this. Playing fair is great, but not when you are dead. The point is, they were able to create a giant that could exist in the night, like the Whytes. This dragon was something else though, it was sentient, and I had the sense it was the thing that was really in charge. We HAVE to be able to find the key to shutting this mist down, otherwise, we are at permanent risk of them breaking through."

"The song singing thing, you are serious about this?"

"It was the deal we made. Tom, Cleath reckons the witches are already into the minds of our people - and with the likes of Hargraves, I can believe it."

"Well, Hargraves thinks he is God, and because you oppose him I suppose it means you are therefore the devil!"

Cliff gives a signal from the pilots' seat, they are coming in to land. Jack laughs, "and this is the Garden of Eden I am corrupting! Tempting the ignorant locals with the evil fruit from the tree of knowledge. That would be about right."

As the hum of the plasma motor died down and the dust they kicked up settled, the doors to the shuttle opened. They were a hundred yards from the wall of mist, pushed back to this point by the resonator. Tom got his first direct sense of the flat emptiness that flowed near to the edge of the two worlds. He pulled the boxes that were stored, opening up the crew to the new suits. "Well, time to get some measurements, and see if the suits let you into their world."

The flitter arriving behind them had the scientific team and the test team, which was Pherial and Cleath, along with a few of the boys out of suits playing watchdog. They were down and pulling out all the measuring gear. "We are going to run actual cable in with you," Tom explained to Jack. "But I will also have wireless monitoring, to see the difference between the two. That alone will give us significant data. This is just a walk in and out, to test the reaction of the suit, please don't get into any arguments before I am done adjusting it."

After they kitted up, Jack, Cleath, and Pherial looked somewhat out of place, with a sort of peaked hat lined with transistors, and the curious vest, grey, but with five nodes around the chest area. Last but not least, Tom pulled out some strange shoes. "Insulators," he explained. "The idea is to have no contact with the ground, just as electricity will earth out, the ionic frequency of these suits will do the same. We need to keep you in the bubble."

After he ran some preliminary tests, he looked over to the tech sitting behind a barrage of field equipment. "Fire it up." he said.

The effect was immediate and strange. Where there had been a grassed plain with trees stretching into the distance, the world around them turned to a clammy dust, like they were in a heavy rainstorm, but without the water. And it seemed heavier, like the gravity had increased. Tom had the equipment power down, and normal vision returned.

"That was unexpected," said Jack. "Looked like we were already in the mist, but it was heavy, clammy, and difficult to see anything bar a sense of dust. This world receded from view and it was like we were in another place."

"Isolating frequencies, you were deprived of input from this range of audible and visual perception. What you saw is a sort of brain mockup," explained Tom.

"I saw the same," said Pherial.

"As did I," added Cleath.

"Shows you how little we know, then," Tom added. "Well, nothing for it but to go into the mist and fire it up there. We are sending you in on a trolley and, like those old fashioned deep sea divers, there is a rope connecting you to back here. Tug on it when you want to be pulled out."

oooOOOOooo

The platform was a sort of rolling stage, not powered. Tom wanted nothing that might interfere with the results. He pushed them into the mist with a small ground unit - Motorized units not reliant on plasma worked in the mist, sufficient for the purpose. Then it came out, leaving the lads to power up, and get a readout.

They were all connected via a main control cable, so Tom could see what they saw, and hear what was around them. He tested the cameras, all was working fine - the small crew stood surrounded by mist, the witch hunters without the 'spacesuit', but carrying nets and copper spears, while Pherial, Jack, and Cleath were all kitted up. The first word as the suits come to life was from Jack. "Wow!"

And it was wow. Instead of mist, as soon as the suits fired up, they were surrounded by technicolor brilliance. All about them, rainbows danced with an effervescence. To the others without suits, it was the same dank mist they had always ventured into, but for those wearing them, everything came alive.

"I can see as they see, at last!" exclaimed Cleath

Even the hard bitten warrior in Pherial softened, "Do you suppose they see our world as that grey dust?" he asked.

"I suppose they do," replied Jack. What he was thinking of was the green and red sunglasses experiment, where you give six strangers the choice of glasses they wish to wear. They go into a room wearing their choice, but the thing is, to those wearing green glasses, the red ones look completely black - you cannot see their eyes. But the eyes of those wearing green glasses are easily seen. The same was true for those wearing the red glasses, the green glass people had black sunglasses, and their 'own' people were easily seen. In the experiment, run many times, on every occasion, the green glass wearing people aligned with their own 'tribe' while the red glass wearing people did the same.

The problem, this world was far more beautiful than their own. He could not have imagined anything more different. This was a place of deep beauty, of peace, and harmony. Dare he say it, a place of freedom. More than this, he felt young, his sense of life was stronger, and an inner part of him understood, in these lands you do not die. A question came to him: *Were those subjugated by witches 'actually' taken over, or had they chosen this world instead of their own?* Rather than make things simple, this experience expanded the level of complication. As Jack had this thought, the face of the golden dragon appeared to form in front of him.

"Your eyes are now open, what do you choose?" it asked, the question piercing his heart with a stark reality.

All of his heart was singing, 'stay here!'. Every fibre of his being wanted to feel this beauty, live in this wonder, be part of the endless bounty that lived all around him. But a small whisper said, no. A tiny voice of cynicism seeped through the cracks of wonder, saying, *"And what sort of song would this make?"*

Without waiting to respond, or seeking to engage the beast, Jack pulled the cord to have them taken out. What a trap, this absolute beauty entranced him, and with all his heart he wished to just stay. He was willing to forget everything he had ever worked for, his people, his purpose. This world was bewitching, truly enthralling. Swiftly, they were drawn from the mist, but for Jack, it was a paradise he was being dragged almost unwillingly from.

oooOOOOooo

The debrief didn't make it any easier. The recordings from their suits showed they had not been subject to hallucination, that the incredible world of color and beauty was real. No dragon head though, that appeared to be a projection. For the present, it was just Tom in the room with the three of them, no one else was seeing this footage.

He was scratching his head, not knowing what to say, so the truth would have to do. "I don't know about you lot, but seeing this makes me want to go there. At the time, I just wanted to live there and forget everything else. Did you all feel the same?"

Cleath was the surprise, "There is beauty everywhere, this is what I always see. The world of the witches, it was very interesting, but what we experienced was because of the suits. For them, perhaps it is real, but for us, this is a dream. Plus, my people are here. I would desire no place they were not."

Pherial agreed, "Of course, it was very pretty. But, our people are here. Life is good, most especially now the mist has moved back. I would not exchange it for such pretty baubles."

"Now I hear people talking sense, I am the same," said Jack, "but if I had not pulled the cord right away, I don't think I would have had the will to do it. For me, it was a paradise."

Tom is blunt, "Let's be real, it is an invasion. It doesn't matter if they are throwing flowers in front of us, it is still an alien race pushing into our world. I look at the footage, and it is incredible, as you say, a paradise - but not for us. It is a paradise for THEM. Everything we humans have carved out since time immemorial is HERE - it means nothing to them there. I would like to put this gently, but we have to sever the tie to that place, or we risk getting lost in it."

"The snake in the Garden of Eden, Tom? What was it you were saying about that?" Jack laughed, half from the relief of escaping that intoxicating beauty, half with regret they had. "But regardless of what is right or wrong, good or bad, HOW do we retain the will to pull out of the mist? That place is hypnotic, it strikes the deepest levels of our brain. I get it, I get why people get entranced by witches - they are given a taste of what we saw and they jettison everything, because of the beauty."

Pherial nods, "And the Whytes, perhaps they think they are saving our people, taking them to a better place. When you consider, they appear not to need to work, to harvest, somehow they live of pure energy in that place. Maybe that IS heaven for some, but for our people, true heaven is where our ancestors wait for us. I do not imagine they wait for us in that mist."

"Master Pherial," Cleath asks, "you spoke of the witches as sending back our people with bits chopped off. That does not sound like a kind of benevolent place. And in the end, an intoxication by beauty is no different to an intoxication with drugs, or power."

"Aye little Cleath, many questions, many questions indeed. How such brutality mixes with such beauty," the Witch Hunter replied.

"One thing is certain," Tom said flatly, "we cannot show this footage to anyone bar Bladwell. For one, they would think we rigged it. The notion of the mist being a paradise is anathema to everything everyone has believed and fought for."

Jack shook his head, "I have to disagree. We do not have the right to prevent people from choosing an alternative path. In fact, I would go further and ask if we can recreate this gear in less cumbersome form, develop it as a sort of simple vest anyone can wear?"

"Yeah, this is just a prototype. Making it smaller was the next step" Tom concurred, but warily.

Cleath was looking at Jack, he felt his thoughts, even though he did not project them. "Tom, we have to give people the option. What you may not understand, if I go there, if I give over to the garden, I don't die. I become the energy, I become the bliss - I have no questions about an afterlife, no need for faith. I am being offered heaven on a stick if I want it. We cannot deny our people this choice."

Tom is shaking his head, "It's too easy. Nothing is that easy, there is a cost you are not seeing, like maybe your eternal soul? Have you ever thought THIS is the deal with the devil? So many will choose the heaven option, and we have few enough humans left as is. People like

Hargraves, he will walk in there, and you know what he will choose ... " This was when the obvious struck home. "Oh, we get rid of people who have an affinity with the witches."

"I didn't say that, Tom. We have discovered a new opportunity, one where your existence is made certain, and we have no right to deny people the choice." Jack had a cryptic smile.

Tom finally understood why DaVinci painted the Mona Lisa.

ooo0000ooo

Bladwell looked at the footage. That was some incredible reversal of expectation. The place was extraordinary. The frequency the witches lived in was stunning, so beautiful that it made their Earth look drab and uninviting - and his first reaction was the same as Tom's - but that would go against everything they stood for. Exploring new worlds, finding the riches therein, this was what every miner looked for in their heart.

But the temptation was obvious, why struggle? Why fight to save an almost dead world when there was a better one waiting on their doorstep? Yes, one where you had to wear an ionic vest to participate in, but by design, they were self-powering and mineral based, so no electronics to break down - at least not for hundreds of years.

The question remained, what happens when you take off the vest? Are you stuck there in the mist, with no way out? What happens if you stay - Do you become a Whyte, a servant to the witches? Not questions you could answer without committing to an existence in the mist. However, Jack made it perfectly clear, under the charter of the Mining Corporation, any form of new riches must be shared with the crew. All have the right to participate in any discovered bounty. It is why you signed on, it is why you left home and family to do the time in space, to gather riches, and to explore.

They were like the sailors of old, setting our across vast oceans in tiny, fragile ships, contending with what the Gods would throw at you. All for the sake of a better life - Well, who could argue that this didn't seem like a better life?

He has Tom on a conference call, but before he invites in the leadership, he needs to be certain. "So, you can create these vests to be more compact, and totally passive - they are powered by the environment? And no questions as to reliability or longevity?"

Tom is not happy, "All of the above, Bladwell - but I don't like it. There is nothing in this that solves any issue we face this side of the curtain. When people will go in, you know a whole batch will stay, and as short-staffed as we are, how can we keep the program up?"

"Agreed, but Jack is right. Our basic charter insists that this discovery is shared. We have to advise the leadership and allow them to fully explore the option."

"Bladwell, it is a fucking DRUG. It is an ILLUSION, a false reality. It is like discovering a poppy field and saying everyone needs to come in and explore it - you know what will happen, they will be stuck there and never leave." Tom hates that he developed the tools for this to happen.

"We have reached the end of our authorization, Tom. It is not for us to decide - we have to hand the baby and the bathwater over to management, and they can choose which one to keep, or otherwise. I expect you to put in a full report, warning people of exactly what you just mentioned - for my part, I agree with you. We are handing over a bomb, not a gift. But it is not our call to make."

"For fucks sake, Bladwell - you KNOW what they will do, send in a research team, and people like Hargraves will be the first to get their greedy little hands on the discovery. I may not like the guy, but I don't want to see anyone live in an eternity of whatever that is in there." Tom argued.

"The choice between Heaven and Hell has always been a personal one, Tom." Bladwell countered.

"But the IRONY - the very people who most opposed everything Blake has been doing out here at the outpost, the ones who protested the most he be replaced, they are the ones most likely to go in and never come out - They are the ones who will happily take the result of his life work and commit to the extinction of their present reality for an unknown, undefined 'heaven'."

Bladwell laughed, "Maybe the real difference between heaven and hell is a sense of irony?" He paused, that was the word for it. "But, not for us to decide. Page Jack and bring him on board for the discussion with the upper echelon."

The meeting lasted but an hour, with the footage being shown, the readouts presented, and a great deal of shock appeared on the faces of those who were in charge of the human race, or what was left of it. Eric Hemus, the chairman, assessed the matter succinctly. "It is a matter for further study and must be handed over to the scientific wing for them to ascertain benefits. There may be a great deal in this, even as a sort of holiday house for the crews. God knows, it is a bleak enough environment for them here, that looks like an excellent place for R&R, provided it proves safe."

"Well, that's the thing," Jack Blake, who had said nothing the entire meeting, spoke. "How do you determine 'safe'? Is it just a question of preservation of life? Let me put it plainly, I am an old man now, very old - even with all the life-extension tricks we have, there is no more than ten years left to this body. But in there, I am young. In there, I will live forever, or so I believe. In there, I have no more responsibility, no more burdens to carry. Plus, it feels so certain. I KNOW this because I feel it. But then I ask myself, *what the fuck do I really know?!* - Seriously, I was prepared to give up my entire life's work to stay in that place."

He paused to let the message sink in, "What you are offering is eternal life. Life eternal in a land of milk and honey, who of us would refuse? How many of us will be left once this door opens?"

Eric shook his head, "It needs to be evaluated. We will send in a hardnosed crew, one not easily swayed, to report on the facts. Plus, we will stay plugged in and do just what you and Tom did, use a wagon we push in and can pull out as and when needed."

"And if they cut the rope, if they unplug? What do you do then?" Jack asked. "You cannot imagine how hard it was for me to tug the rope to be pulled out, and after I did, all I wanted to do was cut it, but I didn't - not for me, but for everyone else. I had no right to decide for them. Plus, who is to say you don't get subjugated by a witch? This could all be an amazingly pretty illusion, a bait to draw in prey."

"Noted, Professor Blake. Your queries and doubts will be added to the file and be included in the study parameters. Gentlemen, we thank you for your service. Is there anything else?"

Jack spoke, "Yes, yes there is, a significant something else. We still have to clear up the mist - for those that choose to stay behind, this planet remains an unholy mess, and those bastards have the key to unlock it. The reason we first went in was to work out if it is feasible to pull out whatever machinery they had that generated the mist. This paradise of plenty is a sidebar, but it risks taking over the main operating parameter for the mission."

One of the scientists spoke, it was Hargraves. "You just want the glory, Blake. We all know this. You accidentally stumbled across what appears to us as a better option, and we thank you for your service, but as to the rest of this matter, it is up to us to decide."

Bladwell intervened. "Not quite, Hargraves. This discovery does not cancel my authority or priorities. Any mission authorized is essentially a field trip and not connected to our main mission, which is to clear up the planet of the ionic mist. I would presume this means finding a way to disconnect our reality from theirs. This means that any who volunteer to go in but get lost in the mist, well, then it will become their new home. There will be no rescue parties. I agree, the whole subject needs further study but at the same time, we are still focussed on cutting off the connection that is creating the mist."

Eric Hemus called the meeting to a close, asking that the minutes note the comments by Mark Bladwell, Chief of Operations, that the scientific party was not part of his existing mission, which remains unchanged. "Thank you, gentlemen, not sure if you handed us a grenade or a bouquet of flowers, but we will set up a mission and keep you advised."

"Before the meeting is called to order, a thing not mentioned which is important," Tom interjected.

"Tom?" Eric was surprised. Junior scientists rarely piped up.

"What about the notion this IS a trap? Some of our best minds will go in there, and we KNOW these witches are telepaths, who could tell if they were taken over? What protocols are in place to verify those we send in do not become patsies for whoever is running that place?"

"This is a valid point being raised, Tom. Jack, can your telepath act as a sort of filter - In some way test those coming out to make sure they are not controlled?"

"To be determined. I see no reason why not, but he IS still just a boy, and I don't want to heap too much responsibility onto young shoulders. Perhaps with his guardian, Pherial Artrim beside him, that could provide a sort of protection - but I have to warn you, if any of our people come out as Whytes, they will be immediately terminated. Plus we need the authorization to quarantine anyone suspected of being infected." Jack emphasized.

The conference call shut down, leaving Jack, Tom, and Pherial sitting in the media room at the outpost, looking at each other. "This will not be the holiday trip those scientists are imagining," Tom said.

Jack was curious, "You didn't feel the desire to stay there, Pherial?"

The great man laughed, his barrel chest heaving with humor, "Stay? All my life is here, Brother Jack. Yes, it was like seeing a pretty girl, you fancy her, but your life is elsewhere. Desire is fleeting in such moments, but I know where my heart lives."

Jack Blake stared for long moments, listening for the hidden message. Everything these people said came from a deep place within them. Then it clicks, "Tom, grounding. You mentioned we had to wear insulating shoes to keep the bubble intact - Can we have a sort of earthing wire in case there is an overload or if a person doesn't want to come back?"

Tom thought about it, "It means we are going to have to do a little more to the suits. These suits are designed to flow ions in a circular motion, and allow a passive interaction - basically to relate to the environment and to pick things up. The design was to develop a suit that got you in there and able to bring back the machinery needed to shut down mist production. A grounding wire is possible, some sort of overload resistor in place that reduces the insulating effect of the shoes. I am not sure of the effect, but it will reduce the ability to interact with the environment."

"Will it be enough to make it look like it does when we are not wearing the suit?" Jack asked.

"Ruin the dream, you mean?" Tom laughed. "The five harmonic points will go out of synch when the grounding effect takes hold. It will prolly interleave as the circuits stabilize, and be a little like living between two worlds, but overall, yes."

"Pherial, what do you think Cleath meant when he said, *'There is beauty everywhere, it is what I see.'* I had the sense he didn't even find the experience in there overly appealing." Jack asked the big man.

"Ah," he sighed, "That child has opened my eyes to so much. Do you know, he sees the mist as beautiful because it insulates him from the noise of people's minds. He would live in there happily if not for the threat of the witches. The boy is a joy and a wonder, the son I always wished for. As to what he meant, it is just as his words said. He DOES see beauty everywhere. He is the optimist, Brother Jack, the eternal dreamer who only sees the best in all."

Jack closed his eyes, allowing his inner vision to come through, "You can show yourself young man."

Cleath appeared, hugging Pherial, "And you are the father I always dreamed of." he spoke with a tear in his eye.

"Do you both understand, in the mist, wearing these suits, this place offers a sort of eternal life? That is heaven in there, a place where beauty, calm, and peace abound. I get that your roots are sunk deep into the soils of your home country, but this place offers a life of ease, without any cares. You can live off the energy of the land itself."

Tom spoke, "And what happens when the energy is sucked completely from the land? This is what I am thinking, that the REASON the witches and their lot want to come to our dimension is exactly for this reason, they have sucked EVERYTHING out of their home soils. To them, HERE is a paradise, a place of virgin energy. We are the only thing standing in their way, because we opened the place back to the sun. When you cannot come into the sunlight, when you cannot take what you want - what do you do? You entice the enemy to your camp.

"Sulla didn't really want to fight the Roman legions sent out by the State to stop him coming into Rome. So what did he do? He set up camp for the Winter and invited the leaders over to have supper, to watch the dancing girls, to talk about their adventures. He gave them everything their hearts desired and in the end, he bought their friendship. Come the Spring, he marched unopposed into Rome."

"If their world is empty, and our world is full, why can we not share?" Cleath asked with all the innocence of youth.

Pherial suggested, "Perhaps they only want to conquer, and sharing is considered too weak a thing to consider."

"But they shared once, with the old race that lived here." Cleath objected. "The old race build houses for them, portals they could visit this world. Songs would be sung to them, prayers would be offered, which gave them the food they needed. In return, they accepted those who went in worship to their special houses and brought them to their world of harmony."

Tom was curious, "Are you talking about the temples of Egypt?"

Jack's eyes gleamed, "And each year, they would do battle between the various houses, a psychic battle, a test of will and heart. I see it, young Cleath. I see what you see!" Then he turned to Pherial, "Do you imagine each clan might erect a temple to house the witches? We can create resonance points, in a sense the reverse of the equipment we used to go to their world, where they can reside." Jack paused, then looked over to Tom, "Can we do this?"

Tom looked at Jack for a long time, "The problem will be the question of whether our people will WANT to. The scientists will go in to inspect everything, and they won't come out. You know this. You know the temptation, the forbidden fruit it offers. Eternal life, paradise! Heaven is waiting for you, all you have to do is kit up and walk into it."

"It was tempting," Jack echoed. "In retrospect, not so much. But right then, right there, I knew in my bones it was a place you didn't die. But BECAUSE of this, it pulled me back. I realized it was a terrible ending to the Song of Trader Jack. Who wants to sing about the guy who gave up all he stood for, everything he fought for, to be willingly swallowed by the mist? It's a bad ending to a long life because there IS no end."

Tom shook his head in opposition. "But those scientists that go in? They won't return. They have made no mark, and have no history worth singing, so they have nothing to lose."

The words of Thoreau came to Jack's memory. It spoke as clearly to him this day as it did back then. "*They honestly think there is no choice left. But alert and healthy natures remember that the sun rose clear. It is never too late to give up our prejudices."*

Jack knew what Tom said was truth. They would not willingly surrender heaven. "Design a suit you can short out, Tom. They will squeal and bitch when their ideal world falls away, but what official complaint can they make? That they wanted to stay there and you stopped them? If we can reach an agreement to clear the ENTIRE Earth of the mist, we will give them what they want - a permanent home, a place where they can feed. My sense is that our people, our songs, our imagination, this feeds them far more than nature. The mist appears to offer eternal life, but in truth, it drains the world of life, of energy, whereas we create it. We are a better long term benefit for them, but lost in paradise, what songs will be sung?

"The witches create the mist as a bridge, what say we give them a place to bridge to? What I am thinking is that we DO build temples, but we call them study centers and let the scientists that love the mist world to become the priests. That way they can plug in to their little heaven, yet still serve their purpose here. The Witch Hunters can perform the yearly ritual of battle, so the Gregorians retain THEIR purpose, and every year we will be given the story of the battle, so a different song can be sung." Jack looks at the other three, seeing if they agree.

A disturbing, sharp female voice came from Cleath's mouth, "This is what my people want, harmony. Yet we need to eat, and your songs will provide us food. We will agree to these terms."

"Cleath? You still there?" Jack asked with a sense of urgency.

His natural voice had returned as he replied, "Yes, I am always here. I just let her speak for her people."

"Pherial, are you in agreement with this plan?" Jack checked with the old man, knowing his word was law with the people.

"Our people will agree. Each clan will build their own temple, and we will sing the song of the day to the witches, as long as the mist is gone and the land is free from their curse," he assented. "But there must be one who will rule over all the clans, who will unite them to this purpose, and adjudicate their grievances."

"The new Pharaoh," Jack whispered. "Cleath?"

A sort of dual voice responded, both Cleath and the witch within him, "We will accept the role as the bridge between the worlds."

Jack patched a call to Bladwell, "We have found the solution to everything!" he exclaimed to the man's incredulous ears.

Master Jack

It's a strange, strange world we live in, Master Jack
You taught me all I know and I'll never look back
It's a very strange world and I thank you, Master Jack

You took a colored ribbon from out of the sky
And taught me how to use it as the years went by
To tie up all your problems and make them look neat
And then to sell them to the people in the street

It's a strange, strange world we live in, Master Jack
You taught me all I know and I'll never look back
It's a very strange world and I thank you, Master Jack

I saw right through the way you started teachin' me now
So someday soon you could get to use me somehow
I thank you very much and know you've been very kind
But I'd better move along before you change my mind

It's a strange, strange world we live in, Master Jack
No hard feelings if I never come back
It's a very strange world and I thank you, Master Jack

You taught me all the things the way you'd like them to be
But I'd like to see if other people agree
It's all very interesting the way you disguise
But I'd like to see the world through my own eyes

It's a strange, strange world we live in, Master Jack
No hard feelings if I never come back
You're a very strange man and I thank you, Master Jack
You're a very strange man and I thank you, Master Jack
You're a very strange man, aren't you, Master Jack?

Epilogue

The story rolled out very much in the way it had been envisioned. Scientists went in to the mist, fell in love with the beauty, then squealed and protested loudly when they were pulled out. This is when the offer was made to placate the scientists by offering the role of chancellor, vice-chancellor, etc. in the new 'universities'. These new complexes were to be a mix, as they were in Ancient Egypt, of school, library, and temple. The clans agreed to the building of these portals on their lands, in return for the mist being withdrawn.

It was the perfect way to educate the natives, feed the witches, and clear the planet.

The mining corporation was able to build the temples, using granite they cut with laser and then floated into place on anti-gravs - nothing so grand as the ancient Egyptian versions, but with sufficient rooms to house a few scientists and a 'house of the holy' set into a luxurious garden. The witches brought into these sacred gardens a sort of stone, one not known to the miners and which they were forbidden to touch. It was the machinery they used to cross the dimensional barrier, and all around each Temple the mist evolved. But everywhere else it dissipated.

The scientists who wanted to live in that world could do so, but only while they were in residence at the temple. The people would come and sing their songs of praise each day, and it didn't seem to matter what they sang about, it was all just food for those within. And little Cleath grew to a man, the leader of all his people, and one who lived between worlds.

When Master Jack and Pherial Artrim eventually moved to their final horizon, songs of their journey were sung in every home, in every temple, and in every heart. The miners took wives, their children were educated in the ways of the old culture and the new - slowly civilization returned.

And so, across the ancient lands, the Egyptian culture arose - Once more, the seed of the new world. Once more. the birthplace for humanity's growth. Once more, the nesting place for creativity and science.

The End

Hunters of the Mist

COPYRIGHT 2021 Ladder to the Moon Publications
Author: Ecallaw Leachim
ISBN: 978-0-6452723-0-7

Publisher: Ladder to the Moon Productions
Email: qrcaustralia@gmail.com
Web: laddertothemoon.com.au

The Wolves of Planet Hope
An Ancient Curse Awakened

It was a shocking discovery, one no-one had suspected. A DNA modifying virus that can be spread with light! Worse, it specifically affected humans and turned them into crazed beasts. Whatever it was on this planet only one thing was certain, it was a threat equal to that which wiped out Old Earth!

It is the Twenty Seventh Century. Mankind has spread out over the galaxy, dominating many worlds in what is called the Federation. But was this one world too far?

Planet Hope, the latest project for the human expansion, is home to a friendly pack of humanoid wolves. They seem entirely welcoming, but soon after settlement, disturbing events required the intervention of the feared Death Squad. A dangerous infection has been found and must be dealt with.

The leader of the squad, Lieutenant Josh Banner, discovers this is no ordinary exercise - He has to assess and deal with a potential threat to ALL humanity, not just the settlement on Hope. Banner looks at the facts and expects only one conclusion – a whole lot of what his squad was named after.

Available on Amazon or at www.laddertothemoon.com.au

"Brilliant - Old Fashioned Sci-Fi at its best!"

Available on
AMAZON

About the Author

Ecallaw Leachim is considered by many to be a polymath. He is accomplished in many diverse fields, as a Master Musician, Master Body Worker, Master Numerologist, Dice Master, Recording Artist, Songwriter, and Publisher. On top of all this he is also a prolific writer with over twenty four titles in print.

www.laddertothemoon.com.au

Aiming for the Stars is much easier if we stop off at the Moon. We are then out of the atmosphere of our past, and can see things more clearly. We are lighter, can jump higher and further than ever before, and it takes far less energy to start each journey.

The hard part is climbing that Ladder to the Moon.